Where
the
Heart
Lays

For My Parents
Raymond and Bonnie Miller
Who give endless support and who
Prove on a daily basis that love exists.

Book 1

Chapter 1

There are certain inalienable truths that guide my life. The first, and one I am most grateful for is that I don't commute. Living in New York City I am afforded the luxury of having my office be ten feet from my bedroom. I write what most people like, fantasy genre with sloppy sex. It's what I'm good at.

Second, I am clumsy. I have no ability to stand in a set place without falling. I actually fell standing still one time. I was at a gallery show with people I didn't know. My literary agent made me go. I had on beautiful black and red Louboutin's, talking with the artist about his inspiration, trying to eat a piece of sushi without getting it on my dress. I managed to shift just so slightly on the five inches between me and the Earth and down I went. Without any elegance I landed on the floor; sadly, the sushi managed to fall with more grace than I did. I have fallen down the stairs, into walls, into furniture, even while walking up the stairs. Heaven forbid someone throw a dog in front of me, I'd fall on it too.

The last truth, the one I most regret, is that I live with the knowledge that I'm an evil person. At least, that's what the voices in my head say. I am the cause of horrific events. The guilt of one action, one bad decision, weighs on me daily; minute by minute there is no escape from its searing pain. It is all consuming. Flashes of desperate moments rush my mind at the oddest of times. The horrors replay and touch my dreams. I cannot move past that Death is a bitch and she has taken a great deal from me.

But Karma, being generous, has balanced out the bitch. Another benefit of writing is that it releases the voices in my head, onto paper rather than onto the populous streets of NYC with a knife and a bad attitude. I couldn't imagine the horror that would roam Stephen King's world if he didn't have such an escape outlet.

At twenty-eight I have four books that have topped the New York Times Best Seller list. The third one Hollywood wanted and they paid gobs of money for it thanks to the negotiating skills of my agent, Anne, the only person in NYC I trust. I've seen the hack jobs Hollywood has done in the past to great books, shredding through authors works, taking a good story and vomiting it out in record time to make money. I didn't want that for my book. I managed to keep a creative influence over the script and the casting; it was the most I could hope for my agent said.

This is what has led me to Hollywood. An expensive dinner, that I don't have to pay for, at seven with the director, the producers and the potential actors and actresses at some fancy-schmancy restaurant I had seen on TMZ a few times.

I'm ready to leave the hotel room by six. I bought a new dress for the occasion, turquoise and body-loving ending just above the knee. My boobs are the main show the dress offers, but in a conservative way. It has short sleeves that end just above the elbows. I'm thin but not Hollywood thin. I hate my skin. I am pale, which seems to be a joke among the few people who know me. I don't tan, I don't even spray tan and as a result I am the palest of pale. Snow White has nothing on me. My only coloring is the endless freckles. I am the Achilles of freckles. I look as if my mother held me by my ankles over the River Freckles and dipped me in. I have a stream of freckles across my face that work their way along my body disproportionately so that I have only a few on my legs. Freckles are only cute on five year old girls.

I have light hazel eyes, a pert little nose and my dark brown hair is a hot mess with a mind of its own. My hair is naturally curly and thick but not the fun kind of curly, it's the hard to work with kind of curly. If I wear my hair short it knots itself into corkscrews which stick out in every direction as if I've stuck my finger in an electrical socket. To keep the horrors of the eighteenth century hairstyles at bay I wear my dark hair long. Most days I wear it in the 'Katniss' style, one long braid down the back. It hangs to just past mid-back and can be contained nicely. On special occasions I break out the flat iron and spend two hours trying to manage it down into a glorious curtain of mahogany. On even specialer occasions I'll take chunks of hair twist it around my fingers and let the ringlets abound.

This was not such a night for the wilds of ringlets so the flat iron is called to duty.

With my hair flat, my nerves on edge and only four inch heels on this time I'm off to the restaurant for the appropriated time. The restaurant is a façade of glass and steel, very modern and kind of cool. It's a good place to be seen acting as if you really don't care to be seen. If a restaurant could be stuck-up this would be a prime example.

A valet opens the cab door and I step out. Paparazzi take a look and continue talking amongst themselves. I smile to myself. I'm glad I don't rate with them. Another valet opens the restaurant door for me. The restaurant is split from the entryway into two sides; to the left is the open floor plan of cozy tables and stark white linens. I square my shoulders and walk to the blonde hostess. She eye fucks me for a second then smiles, "How may I help you?"

"I'm with the Breckanger party. Are they here yet?" Todd Breckanger, Hollywood's go-to guy. He is the equivalent of finding a leprechaun at the end of the movie rainbow, everything he touches is gold and he will be my producer for the movie.

"Mr. Breckanger's assistant called and said they'll be about thirty minutes late. Mr. Dash has arrived as well," she smiles almost dreamily when she mentions his name, "he's in the bar. May I show you?"

4

I nod. Thirty minutes, what am I going to do for thirty minutes?

I follow the hostess to the right and enter the bar. Gone are the linens. The tables are smaller; the chairs huskier. A few flat screens, hung on the walls, are strategically placed for entertainment purposes. At the rear is the bar which expands across the room with taller chairs that mimic the weightiness of the others. And there he is, sitting with his back to me. My heart skips a beat as I follow the hostess through the maze of tables and people to the bar.

"Mr. Dash," she says sweetly, "Another member of your party, sir."

My eyes follow the genuine smile she gives him. He nods and looks from her to me. I had seen his movies and knew what to expect but he is more in every way.

Ethan Dash, an all American man from somewhere in Pennsylvania I found out from my research. I'd spent countless hours over the last few weeks researching everyone I would meet tonight, everyone who might have a hand in how my work will be interpreted onto the big screen. He is a little older than me at thirty-one, broad shoulders, lean waist. His hair is the color of wheat, pushed to the side as if the wheat is waving in the wind. He has never played a role in a drama, yet the films he has starred in totaled almost a billion dollars in receipts. He smiles at me and I suddenly know why so many people go to the

movies to see him. He is handsome in a button-up
navy shirt and dark gray linen pants. He offers me the
seat beside him, "You must be the writer." I nod,
aware that I cannot form words yet. He sets his beer
down and offers his hand in greeting. His touch is
warm before I blink myself awake.

"Yes, I'm Lauren Radford, the writer." I scoot
up onto the seat beside him and turn my attention to
much needed alcohol. The bartender stops for a
moment and I order, "I'll have a glass of Riesling, house
is fine." He pours me a glass and I ask, "Do you have
any nuts?" There's a stifled laugh from beside me and
a smirk from the bartender. I look at Mr. America
disapprovingly and proclaim, "I haven't eaten all day.
I'm gonna faint if I don't eat something now."
Between traveling and doing my hair the day was shot.

"A woman who eats, that's not something I
thought I'd see in Hollywood." Ethan raises his beer
bottle slightly, "Cheers." I take a long pull from my
wine. Tasty...a little too tasty. I think I'll have another
as soon as this one's finished.

I take a minute to follow his stare to the TV set
behind the bar. It's a pro game and I let slip, "The
Falcons are good this year. No one would've expected
that."

Ethan eyes me critically, "You like football?"

"I love college ball, the pros are OK." Another
chug of wine, a handful of nuts to ease my pain. "My
favorite team is Alabama," I smile, "Roll Tide." I can't

figure out why I'm so chatty but continue, "I like all sports. Just not cricket, I can't figure out the rules." His smile returns, I must amuse him.

There's an obnoxious roar from behind me so I turn to look, and groan. Cole Arrington, GOD in human form, has arrived. Ethan jumps from his chair and bear-hugs the other man for a moment. I yearn to be in the middle of that man-sandwich. Cole is the superhero type that one of the casting agents wants. He's Australian, heavily accented, long sandy blonde hair and built like a brick wall with the look of a surfer. He's a little taller than Ethan and better dressed, if that's possible, in a dark suit, white shirt and no tie.

"This is the writer Lauren," Ethan says.

I scoot from the chair and offer my hand to Cole. He clasps it a little too enthusiastically with a friendly hello. I manage a greeting before returning to my seat. They're loud together, talking of things that have passed, of things that have come to be and I remember they'd made a movie together a few years ago. From what I found online, Cole's happily married to one of the most beautiful women in the world. Literally, she was Miss Universe a few years ago. They have a beautiful little boy and another on the way. Cole orders a beer from the bartender and the men focus on the game.

The voices in my head resurface and remind me that I don't like new people or new places and I begin to feel the crawl of lunacy around my neck again. The sudden anxiety is intense. My heart is racing. I don't fit in here. I don't fit in anywhere. I shouldn't have left New York a voice says from deep inside me. The others agree.

I gulp the last of the wine and take a bill from my clutch. I agree with the voices, I've made a mistake. I need to leave. I slide off of the chair and turn to go. The guys will never know I've left; they're focused on the game. I can call Anne from the hotel and tell her to tweak the contract. The studio can have full rights to it. I'm out of my league.

I grip my bag harder. As soon as my heels touch the floor I step away. I'm just able to stop in time, finding a mass of masculinity behind me. The last of the actors has arrived and I think my mouth hits the floor.

"Whoa," escapes my lips and he smiles. It's a smile that caresses his smoky blue eyes. The Swedish import. I'd rented every movie that had his name in it over the last month and saw his talent along with his abs of steel. He started in small roles and has moved up to larger supporting roles. My movie will be his chance at a leading role.

I knew what to expect but seeing him in person takes my breath away. He's very tall and lean but all muscle. His short, recently trimmed hair is dirty blonde and he's every bit a Nordic deity. I need to congratulate his parents on having sex at the precise moment for his conception.

He's wearing a gray three piece suit, (do men wear three piece suits anymore?), with a sharp white shirt and a dark purple tie. He is disarmingly beautiful but in ways the other men aren't with his clean-shaven rugged jawline, sculptured lips and a straight nose that I suddenly want to plant a kiss on.

"Going somewhere?" he asks as if he knows my inside joke and I make a noncommittal sound offering my hand. I can't be rude. Not to him. Taking his hand I feel the shockwave of his warm touch all the way to my hoochie. "I'm Willem Rysberg, please, call me Will," he says then leans forward and kisses my cheek. I rise slightly to meet his touch. I swear even my breasts perk up and pay attention. My eyes close slightly and he smells, my eyes flash open, he smells wonderfully like home and my senses come alive.

Home…home…home.

It's been so long since I've smelled the aroma of home, my real home. I flush with heat instantly at the spot where his lips touched. Fortunately, my freckles act like camouflage.

"Lauren," I manage to get out as our hands fall apart. He's thirty-five, so said his online bio and from the gossip sites I've learned he's a player. Different women, different cities, countries. He is a globe-trotting horn-bag. He probably keeps the condom makers in business all by himself. A voice taunts deep from within, wondering about restaurant sex with him. Would he be willing? I could sit on the chair behind me...that would give me some height. He could unzip those pants and we could get down to business. Caught in my own sexual dilemma I don't even notice as the hostess approaches.

"Pardon me," she announces with great ease. I hate her instantly. "Your party has arrived. If you'll follow me," she turns to lead the way. Cole and Ethan grab their beers and follow. I am intensely aware of my being with Willem walking behind me. Am I standing up straight? Are there any road hazards in my path? Am I going to fall? How does my butt look in this dress from behind? I can't keep my thoughts organized and press my fingers to a sore spot on my temple. I need medication or another glass of wine.

Sitting at a large round table with a delicate white linen cloth over it near the rear of the restaurant I have my back to the wall looking out at the main room. This way no one can sneak up from behind and surprise me.

The actresses have arrived, nearly all at one time. Overwhelming. I keep reminding myself that I knew this would be difficult. I knew I would be surrounded by beautiful people and that my self-esteem would take a hit. I just didn't realize how painful that would be.

They are striking and I'm as green as my dress with envy. Their bodies are killer, with clothes made to drape over every surgically enhanced curve. Their hair and makeup have been done by professionals. Nothing has been left to chance. I am reminded of ancient lore of the three sirens and their seductive songs. I sigh and place my napkin in my lap.

Todd is to my left and Willem has taken the seat to my right. As I am pale, Todd is tan. He needs to take a break from the tanner; I'm a little worried for him. His dark hair is marked with streaks of gray. Thick eyebrows sit like caterpillars over his brown eyes and his nose has the look of being broken more than one time. His teeth seem exceptionally white against the tan and I'm momentarily caught in the daze. I silently vow not to tan. He's talkative and energetic. I like him immediately.

I am introduced to each of the others but I'm already sitting so I give a simple wave as we go around the table. The director, Josh Wheaton; he's young for a director, kind of geeky looking with super short brown hair and dark-rimmed Harry Potter glasses resting on his face, is seated next to Todd and they talk of everything but my movie. Todd's co-producer is Nicole Jackson; she's half his age with beautiful light brown skin and does a great deal of work based on how much her phone pings during our introduction. She says she's glad to meet me and I'm sure she's just glad to meet the money my movie will make her.

I nod to the actors having met them already. Ethan, the movie brawler. Cole, the movie superhero. The ladies are next as we go around the table. Three in a row, all dark haired beauties, all just barely over twenty-one: Holly, Kate and Maria. I view them as a scientist would view specimens in a petri dish. I have my own vision of my female character, do they conform? Or do I need to conform to them? Suddenly I ask, "The female character has short hair, are you going to cut yours?"

They each look from one to the other and Kate says, "I would, for the role."

I lean back slightly in my chair and stiffen to ramrod straight. She's given me a line, that as an actor, she would do whatever was necessary for the role. I could have asked her if she'd be willing to take it up the ass and I would have gotten the same response. Maria mumbles something about wigs and good lightening, no one would know. Huh? I would know. And I shut up.

Willem sits next to me, he's relaxed and easy-going, and everything I am not. I glance up and take in his splendor. He weakens my resolve to run. Sitting next to him, smelling so good like a woodsy outdoorsman who bathed in spice, my determination is fading fast.

I sit and watch as the waiter takes our orders; the ladies will have salads. A variety: one with spinach, one with only lettuce. Only lettuce? How boring. Kate breaks the trend and orders grilled chicken on her salad. My shoulders slump, I feel fat. I order a small steak and some golden fried potatoes and green

12

veggies for good measure. Ethan catches my eye and winks, making a face from across the table, reminding me of what he said earlier, that women in Hollywood don't eat.

Josh takes a minute from Todd's attention and asks me, "Lauren, I'd love to know how you came up with the story?" I set down my second glass of wine. Everyone is looking at me. I hate being the center of attention.

"It was a dream," which sounds so much better than one of the voices in my mind kept reminding me of a particular idea and wouldn't give up on it until it was written down. "I think I dreamt about it for three or four nights in a row then starting writing out the story."

Maria adds, "I love that you put a love story in the middle of an invasion. It was so romantic, him saving her from the ocean."

"Thank you," what else can I say? "They say write what you know," I shrug.

"You know about invasions?" Ethan laughs.

"No, I had to research that part. I know about fear." And everyone gets quiet for a long minute. Awkward.

Willem leans close, his voice is rather low as the others begin to talk amongst themselves, "My mom loves your books. She's the one who told me to try for the role."

"I'm glad she likes them. I can sign a book for her if you want." He leans back with an enigmatic smile. I think he's accepted my book offer. I don't know why but I keep talking, "Let her know I have another book coming out next year, in the spring. I finished it last month. It's at the editor's right now."

Todd looks at me, under his paternalistic scrutiny I shrink, "I'd like a first copy too. I want to keep the studio's options open on your books, if the movie does well." They're judging potential movie sales based on my book sales. Even if half the people who bought my book go to the theatre, they'll have a blockbuster. I know it, Anne knows, that's why she was able to get so much money for the rights. She wants me here, wants me watching over the creative process. She's as protective of my book as I am, and I love her dearly for it. For her...and the Nordic deity, I guess I'll stay.

There's chitchat and banter and lots of giggling from the young ladies. The guys are talking of sports and families and everyone is so friendly. I can't decide if it's genuine friendly or phony friendly. I smile a few times, trying to keep up with all of the different conversations. This is what it must be like to have a family. To sit around a table and eat and enjoy each other's company, talk of the old days and what is to come. I rub the sore spot that appears again at my temple as Holly asks, "Will, are you Swedish, or you know, is your old family from Sweden?"

14

He smiles and answers, "I am Swedish, I grew up in Stockholm."

"Jag växte upp I Stockholm också," I blurt out in Swedish. My fork drops to my plate with a loud rattling clank and my hand covers my mouth. *I grew up in Stockholm also.* Willem looks at me as if I'm glowing like a light bulb. I haven't spoken a word of Swedish in eleven years. Eleven years. I could never tell any of them what happened. Fear, I know about fear. I look to Willem and can't gauge his reaction.

Asked...to...leave.

I can't be near him when he reminds me of home, a place I can't return to.

"You speak Swedish?" Kate asks in wonder as Holly asks, "Are you Swedish too?" The table stops talking and focuses on me.

I shake my head and revert to using English only, "No, I just lived there when I was a kid." I pick up my fork again and try to refocus on my food but I've lost my appetite. My fucking hand is shaking. The fork is trembling like we're having an earthquake. I hope no one notices. All of the voices in my head are screaming at me for the stupid mistake. I can't keep the voices at the table apart from the ones in my head as everyone talks/screams at once. "Excuse me," I say as I stand. I have to leave, I need some air.

The alley is nice, for an alley. There are lots of alleys in NYC and it's kind of homey standing in the dark while the activity of the busy restaurant passes me by. I can hear the commotion but am not a participant. The waiter propped open the door for me so I'm not five feet from the inside but it's enough to get away. The night air is calming the angry voices.

I'm pushing a stone across the concrete with the toe of my shoe when he asks me, "Are you coming back in?" Looking up I see some emotion, like measured apprehension, on Willem's face. "You can't let them know they get to you, if that's what's wrong." No accent, not even a hint. He's spent a lot of time speaking English.

I shrug and walk to him, "I'm okay. I just needed some air." He steps aside and I brush past him. A gentle hand on my shoulder and my body shocks awake again. His firm hand slides along my back, resting on my hip as we walk side by side back towards the main room. His touch is warming and comfortable. I can forgive his whoreness.

He leans in and says, "Hollywood is all about pretending, or acting, as some say." He smiles for me and my insides melt into goo. "Remember as a kid when you pretended to have fun with your family on holiday or you pretended to eat your dinner so you could watch TV, same thing here. Just pretend you're having fun."

I ask one word, "Why?"

He replies, "Because these people are going to spend nearly a hundred million dollars to make a film

16

based on your imagination, give them your time and attention." He presses a light kiss to my dark hair before leaning away. We arrive at the table and he pulls out my chair for me. I sit down and smile at the group. There is an apology for wasted time and everyone is cheerful again.

Chapter 2

Grateful for the good food and the cool, late September night air I stand in front of the restaurant and spy on Willem. Wow, he is so attractive! He's passing over his valet ticket trying to get his car out of hock. I'm talking with Nicole about the schedule for tomorrow but not really paying attention. Nicole glances over her shoulder, sees where I'm looking and smiles, "Cute, isn't he?"

I mumble, "They're all cute." But cute really isn't the right word to describe the men I've spent the evening with. Door-busters, men on whom Hollywood can count on to return their investment, make the ladies swoon, give 'em someone to dream of at night.

She returns my smile, "I'll email you the schedule."

I say my goodnights to everyone and watch the paparazzi follow the ladies as they continue their night on the town. I'm again glad that I don't rate with the press. I'd hate to be stuck in their fishbowl of ever examining eyes. It's enough for me to be unbalanced and crazy. I don't need people photographing me losing my mind. I turn from the restaurant and start to walk back towards the hotel. From the cab ride earlier I know it's only three or four blocks away, easy walking for a New Yorker.

The night air is soothing my mind and I need it. The occasional palm tree planted next to the sidewalk and the smell of the ocean remind me that this is not my city. The hum of an engine seizes my attention as it pulls up next to me. The passenger window slides down and I hear someone call my name. I stop and look, catching Willem's silhouette outlined by the dashboard light. I step to the edge of the sidewalk and lean down to talk. It's a high-end white Maserati and the engine is almost purring as it rests.

"Hi there," I say.

He's not smiling; in fact, his eyes aren't even focused on mine. For longer than what's polite, his eyes focus on my breasts. The girls are putting on a good show as I lean to the car window. I snap my fingers and get his attention.

He smiles that killer crooked smile of his and I have to laugh, "You know I look like a prostitute out here."

His smile gets even bigger, "Then get in before the cops bust us."

As soon as I'm in and buckled up he pushes the car into the nighttime traffic and asks, "Have you ever been to LA?" I murmur that no I haven't and am rewarded with another crooked grin. "Do you really want me to drive you back to your hotel?" he asks salaciously and I get the impression he's asking something else.

"What do you have in mind?" I am such a want-to-be slut.

"I know somewhere fun," he glances over his shoulder and changes lanes.

He really does mean somewhere fun. He parks the Maserati in front of the Santa Monica pier. Colorful lights are pulsing through the darkness, keeping beat with the music that's playing over the loudspeakers. People seem to be everywhere, even though the hour's late. He takes a minute and removes his tie, tossing it into the center console next to my clutch. A few buttons of his white shirt are undone as he makes himself comfortable, I just watch in fascination. He finishes and asks me, "Are you ready?" I smile shyly, sure that I really am ready for anything he has in mind, and exit the car.

He changes out a twenty for ones before we walk into the arcade. I haven't been in an arcade in what feels like a hundred years. The air smells sweet like cotton candy. There are games in every direction. The neon lights dance over the walls and the music is too loud. He hands me some ones and we pick our first game to play, "Whack-A-Mole". I realize, as I'm missing the little moles with the oversized padded mallet, that I am as uncoordinated with my hands as I am with my feet. I miss more than I hit and he enjoys his little victory. I do better with the water pistols but still lose miserably. I sulk and pout.

He laughs and his voice is rich and masculine, his smile reaching those smoky blue stunning eyes. We play a few more games, wherein I lose all of them. He takes my hand and leads me from the arcade. He asks, "Are you hungry? You want some popcorn?" Dinner was filling so I tell him thanks but no thanks. There's a promise of fried dough later on, if I want it. I can only think of all the things I could do with him and powdered sugar, and I beam.

We walk away from the dancing lights and he drops my hand. Our arms occasionally touch reminding me of our exhilarating connection as we walk side by side along the darkened pier. My hair whips in the ocean breeze. I try to bring it under control by grabbing it with my hands but give up on the losing battle after a minute.

"Are you cold?" he asks. I am slightly but before I can say no he takes off his jacket and slips it over my shoulders. His jacket smells like him and I'm comforted by it and its warmth as I tuck my arms into the long sleeves.

Willem stands at the end of the pier looking out into the dark ocean. The salty air of the sea has replaced the sugary smell. His hands grab hold of the old wooden barrier before he turns back to me and I step closer, joining him at the railing. He seems almost shy as he asks, "You grew up in Stockholm, huh?" I shrug and stand beside him looking out into the endless darkness. "Where did you live? You still speak well." He turns back and we stand shoulder to shoulder, touching, gazing out over the murky ocean. "Tell me about your time there."

He's asking a lot of me but he doesn't know it. I start with the small things, "Do you know the candy shop that's on Snickarbacken?"

"That hasn't been there for years. I think it's a coffee shop now."

"Well, that's just as good." Candy for adults. He looks at me for a long moment waiting patiently for me to continue. Finally I do, saying, "My parents and I used to live near there. It was more their base of operations." I smirk at the memory. "I used to go to the International School over on Johannesgatan. I could walk there from our apartment." The ocean breeze changes and my hair pulls away from my face.

"I know that school. My family lives closer to downtown."

"Your family still lives there?"

He nods and smiles, "All of my family are there...grandparents, mom and dad. I have two brothers and three sisters. They all live there too."

"Wow!" I'm astonished and laugh, "You have a big family!" I'm still laughing and ask, "Are you the youngest? Oldest?"

"Oldest. How about you?"

I shrug, "I'm the youngest of three. I'm a change of life baby," his brow furrows and I explain,

"My parents were old when I was born. I was a mistake, an accident."

"A surprise," he shifts closer so that our shoulders are touching.

"Maybe," I like having him close. "My parents were retired. They wanted to travel the world and didn't want me to hold them back. Stockholm was where I stayed. Not them, not my brothers. My brothers were almost thirty when I was born so we aren't close. Both of my parents have passed now so I don't really have any family."

"And you live alone in New York?"

I nod, "One of my brothers is in Mississippi, in and out of jail. I try not to talk with him, he's always in trouble." I have enough trouble of my own.

"Why's your brother in jail?"

"Stupid stuff, he bounced checks, got a DUI, robbed a convenience store. Oh, please don't hold that against me." I have no excuse for his actions. I am not my brother's keeper.

"I won't," and there's a bit of a grin on his divine lips.

"My other brother lives in Chicago with his family. We just aren't close."

"Do you get lonely by yourself?" he asks.

How can I get lonely with all the voices in my head? "Most of the time, no, I don't. I've been so busy with my writing and establishing my career since I graduated college. I have the storylines for seven more books sitting on my computer just waiting for me. I don't have much time for breaks between books. It doesn't leave much time for," I shrug, "me." I need to clarify something, "Please let me explain, at dinner," he's listening intently, his beautiful eyes caressing me and I'm momentarily lost within the depths of smoky blue. I blink myself back to awareness, "I got overwhelmed. I don't spend much time with people, it's an occupational hazard. Everyone was talking and I couldn't keep up. Plus the voices in my head wouldn't shut up," I laugh half-heartedly as if it's a lame joke.

"I understand. This town can be overpowering." He's quiet for a long moment before he asks, "Who did you stay with in Stockholm since your parents traveled so much? How long did you live there? I just want to know if we could have met when we were younger."

"I stayed by myself. I moved back to the US before I turned eighteen." I smile but I've lost some enthusiasm, I don't want to talk about home. I push away from the pier railing and take a step back towards the distant lights.

He follows next to me, "You really impressed me, just speaking up like that. I like knowing I can talk with you."

My heel drops suddenly between the planks, my stomach lurches. I'm hopping on one foot and stretch out my hand for his. "Wait! Wait!" The words rush, "I'm stuck!" He takes my hand to keep me balanced. I look up as I bend down, "My heel's stuck."

"Let me help," and he steps closer, holding my hand tightly. I wiggle my foot out of the stuck heel and hop around in just the one. I know this is dangerous considering the level of clumsiness I'm capable of. I hold onto his hand and wiggle out of the other shoe as he tugs my heel free from the plank. "Your shoe, my lady." He's so serious I burst with laughter and am awarded with a devilish grin. I take both shoes in one hand and hold his warm hand with the other. Barefoot I walk along the pier next to him and step up onto the old wooden bench to look over the edge.

I'm flirting with danger.

He grabs my hips with both hands to steady me. "Don't do that," he says.

I glance over my shoulder and give him a breathtaking smile, "Are you worried?"

"I don't even know if you can swim and I really don't want to jump in after you." I turn to him and reassure him that I can. I am only slightly taller than he is. Willem is really tall, or I am really short or both. He says, "I don't even like you walking barefoot." He looks warily at the pier, "You never know what's on the ground." He presents his back to me, "Let me give you a," he stops and looks over his shoulder, "What's the English word?"

"Lift? Piggy back ride?" I giggle.

25

His smile returns full watt and takes my breath, "Yes, a piggy back ride, come." It's the first time I hear a bit of an accent in his words. I laugh and I lean onto his back. I wrap my arms around his neck and shoulders. He takes my legs and hikes me further onto his back. I swing my legs as he walks the rest of the pier. I feel such freedom, acting my age. I hadn't realized the heaviness of oppression that I had on my soul until he let me have some fun.

He walks with me all the way to the Maserati and backs up to the hood. I release my arms from his shoulders and sit on the car. I have an idiotic grin on my face. He retrieves the car keys from his pants pocket and opens the passenger side door. I go to get off of the hood and he scoops me up easily. I giggle again at the surprise. He sets me gently into the passenger seat and closes the door. I feel like a complete idiot being so happy. As he walks around the car I take off his jacket and set it in the seat behind me.

I watch him but look around the car as well. It's hideously late. The arcade lights are off, leaving the building in shadows. There are just a few people around, fewer cars. Willem folds himself easily into car as he gets in. Such grace, I'm envious since I can't even walk down a pier and back. He turns to me and looks uncertain. He seems to be thinking of many things at one time. He hesitates for a moment so I shift in my seat. I lean across him and brace myself on his door and shift until I am straddling him, face to face in the driver's seat. This is the best way to talk, but I really don't have talking in mind. His hands fall to my hips then caress my back. His touch is making me hypersensitive.

I lean forward and press my lips to his, hesitantly, waiting for any kind of response from him. The gentle kiss turns hard and demanding as his hand travels up my back and twines my hair into his fist. My eyes close in pleasure. His lips are like pure ecstasy. My tongue darts into his mouth and he tastes of a trace of the beer he was drinking with dinner. I lean closer crushing my breasts against his chest. His other hand presses against my hips and I feel his growing erection as I straddle him. A moan escapes my lips. He accepts the sound as permission and holds me hard against him. Our lips are tangled; my hair has enveloped us blotting out the world.

"You are so beautiful," he says pushing my hair back. His accent has vanished; his words are perfect again. His eyes are full of ache and desire, and I know I'm returning the look. His fingers frame my cheek and he pulls me closer for another kiss. I want him so badly; my body is trembling with desire.

Another kiss, gentle and seductive, takes my breath. My lips swell beneath his passion. I haven't been kissed like this in years, maybe never. His hands move beneath the skirt of my dress. His fingers stroke my thighs softly as they travel up to my hips then along my backside tracing the outline of my thong.

I hear a hiss from behind. A ghost is creeping around my mind. It's digging into my mind, tossing brain matter everywhere, pulling me from the moment. It hisses two words in my ear, 'casting couch' and I freeze. The other voices are chipping away at my sanity, agreeing with the other. Am I the couch? How much influence does Willem think I have over the choices for the roles? He's a well-known whore but would he do this for a role? I lean back, breaking the connection.

"I don't want to do this here," he's almost short of breath. "Can I take you home? Or back to your hotel?"

"Do you think this will get you the job?" I ask maliciously. "A good fuck for the writer and you'll get the role?" I crawl off of him back into the passenger seat. I put on my shoes and grab my clutch.

"What the fuck are you talking about?" He goes from zero to angry in a nanosecond. "I've never fucked for a role, and I'm not starting now." He runs his hands through his dirty blonde hair, "I think you're beautiful and smart and...," he's lost the words.

"Good, fucking for a job is just beneath you," I snap. "Cause I can't give the job to you," it sounds almost like an imploration. "I don't have that much influence over who they choose. You'll have to earn it!" I'm shouting and I hate shouting. It reminds me of the voices. They unleash their fury on my brain, screaming, tormenting me. I am a whore, a killer to them, they'll never let me forgot it. I pull open the door latch and nearly jump out. I'm outta here.

He's out of the car just as fast, "Where the hell are you going, Lauren?"

I cast him an angry look, the best I can muster and stalk towards the last cab sitting at the pier. I nearly throw myself into the cab and watch Willem standing there in the parking lot as the cabbie drives away.

What the hell did I just do? I lean back into the seat, all the anger, all of the passion gone and I'm left an empty shell of the person I used to be.

Chapter 3

I cannot sleep. I'm restless all night alone in my hotel room. I knew I owed him an apology before streams of sunlight filtered through the room window. I just got upset thinking I was being used. The fucking voices didn't help much either. His reaction should have calmed me. He was completely pissed at the insinuation. He doesn't fuck for roles. He wanted me, not my influence. He wanted me, and I'm awestruck by the idea. I wonder if he still might and comprehend that's just not a possibility. Whatever was to be with him is gone. Willem is not the kind of man who will wait. Especially for a woman like me.

I check my emailed schedule and find that today I view the actors' auditions. It's taken months to narrow down their search to the few people I met last night. Nicole and Todd have set it up, it's all planned; now I just have to show up and decide. One pair: female lead and male lead acting together, paired by Nicole and the casting agents; each with whom they think has the right spark. The chemistry that lovers have. I sigh regretfully. I would have liked to have had some of that chemistry. The script is set; they'll go through the lines. Once the decision is made they'll move forward with making contract offers, the offers for the actors with minor roles and the filming schedule.

Nothing starts before ten so I have a lazy breakfast and set the tray of dirty dishes in the hall outside my room. After my shower I braid my wet hair in the everyday style. I put a little eye makeup on but leave off the concealer; the freckles cannot be concealed or contained. Freakish monsters that they are. I'm in my best blue jeans, a white t-shirt and some wedge sandals. They feel safer to walk in than any of the heels I have in my luggage. I dump the contents from my clutch into my regular purse and head for the door with thirty minutes to find a cab and get to Nicole's house.

The cab pulls up to Nicole's house, which I would call a heavily-Spanish-influenced small mansion, with ten minutes to spare. The studio had offered a private driver for the week I'm in LA but I couldn't see the use of some guy bored out of his mind while he waits to drive me around. Cabs work in New York; they can work in this city too. I pay the man and get out. There's a tall metal gate surrounding the property but the driveway gate is open so I walk through. There are plenty of sports cars parked in the round driveway but no white Maserati and I take a deep breath, relaxing. No apologies forthcoming.

I ring the doorbell and stand for just a moment before Nicole opens it with a big smile on her face. *Am I on TMZ?* I can't help but ask, "Why the smile?" I'm silently praying I haven't been filmed on someone's

31

cell sexually attacking one of Hollywood's most eligible bachelors. My street cred would go into the gutter. I could never pick him, not in a million years, even if he was the best actor for the job if anyone knew what we had done in the car. The movie would always be tainted with innuendo and gossip.

She takes me in a big hug, very un-Nicole-like and pulls me into the house. A margarita is in one hand and she offers it to me. I decline so she sips it, "I'm so happy this morning," she says in a way that makes her appear ten years younger. "News of your," OH GOD! Not my teenage make-out antics! I'm going to faint on the spot! "next novel coming out got picked up by outlets," I breathe. This isn't about the kissing and touching and...my mind drifts. Happy thoughts, pleasant memories. Refocusing...I think she means news outlets, "Someone must have spilled the beans after you mentioned it at dinner last night, which is a great thing. No such thing as bad publicity, right? Everyone at the studio is buzzing about it." She leans close and lowers her voice, "Todd said he'd give me a bonus if I can get a pre-print copy from you." She's walking as she's talking, leading me into the house. "Don't worry, I won't bother you about it, just keep me in mind, OK?" She's still smiling; it must be the margarita and the promise of a bonus. I put fainting on the Do Later list.

Her house is beautiful, neatly arranged and professionally organized. From the entry hall we come into her main living room. My whole apartment is the size of her living room, well almost. The back wall has a stone fireplace which takes up most of the wall and there are two large dark leather couches that face each other in front of it. Lots of red and gold pillows are scattered on the couches, which match the red and gold pattern on the enormous area rug. Off to the right is the open kitchen. It seems to have the best of everything in it. Sitting on tall stools at the counter is Ethan and Kate. He's mixing drinks with a blender. This is to be a casual event.

"Hi everyone," I say with a smile and walk into the kitchen. I drop my purse onto the granite counter top, away from the blender and step closer. Time to be friendly.

Without the other actresses around to intimidate me I find that I like Kate. She's very pretty and has been an actress since she was a kid when her mom got her a job in a laundry soap commercial. I never saw the commercial, living overseas, but the others nod and agree as if they remember the TV spot.

After a few minutes I ask Nicole if she has a bottle of water and she points to the fridge. I walk over and open the right side metal door. I grab one and return to my designated spot close to my purse and wait for the others to take the lead.

Todd, Josh and a few other people, that I'm quickly introduced to and just as quickly forget their names, join us before we get down to business. I grab my iPad and stylus from my purse, my water bottle and follow the others out of the kitchen, past the living room, a step down into a small foyer area. On the right are a set of stairs to the second floor but we take the hall just past the stairs and work our way to another large room. It is spartanly filled with just a few chairs and smaller couches. It's stark compared to the rest of the house. This is definitely a work room. I'm relieved to realize that it's not all margaritas and fancy dinners. There will be real work done for my movie.

I pick a seat on a far couch, put stylus to screen and get ready to be schooled. I have nothing to contribute, so I don't talk for an hour as the audition continues. Nicole and Todd throw out their opinions as if it's second nature. Josh is much more hands-on as he literally takes Ethan and Kate by the hands and moves them here and there. We watch them go through a few scenes. It is an odd feeling to know the words that come out of their mouths as intimately as I do. They are wonderful together; they create an ebb and flow within their work. I can't help but clap as the audition comes to an end. Ethan turns to me with a wink and gives me an embellished Shakespearian bow. I have pages of notes about each of them.

"Good job Ethan and Kate, we'll be in touch." Todd says with a million watt white smile, "You'll have to leave now so we can talk about you two behind your backs."

There are handshakes and kisses on the cheek before they leave. Someone has ordered lunch and I am treated to a grilled chicken salad. I go over my notes as Todd, Nicole and Josh talk around the kitchen table. They're evaluating the acting, point by point. It really does feel as if we're talking about them behind their backs. Everything is taken into account about Ethan and Kate, even that her last movie didn't make the money the studio thought it would. Todd tells us that it would be difficult for the studio to place the enormity of the part on her with such a poor past performance. Logistical questions are proposed and written down, needing to verify information with others.

Nicole looks at me, "We're trying to set the schedule for next summer, to film in Hawaii. Will you come with us? At least for a week or two?" I smile and agree. I can make time to go to Hawaii.

Thirty minutes later Holly arrives for her audition with Willem. She is very nice but I don't like the way she flirts and jokes around with Josh. I'm fidgeting, waiting for Will's arrival. It feels like I'm waiting for an executioner, my apology hangs like a guillotine blade over my fragile ego. My pulse goes through the roof when I think I hear the Maserati. I sure I'm imagining that I hear his footsteps and then the doorbell rings.

I jump from the couch and announce too loudly, "I'll get it," before anyone else has a chance to move. Nicole notices my anxiety and eyes me curiously. I can get nothing past her. I open the door and there he is, just as good looking as the previous night, in jeans and a dark green V-neck t-shirt. There is a whisper of golden chest hair peeking out from the deepest part of the v. I groan internally, he could have been mine.

He smiles hesitantly when he sees me. "Hello Lauren," he says testing the waters, being very polite. I'm not going to explode, if that's what he's worried about, in fact I feel rather ashamed of how I acted.

He starts to come in and I press my hand against his chest stopping his progress. His wonderful, muscular chest underneath my hand...but I digress. I glance over my shoulder quickly and see the others are busy so I step outside and close the door behind me. He steps back, making room for me on the porch.

"Do you have something to say to me?" he asks.

In for the pound I start, "I want to apologize,"

He stops me, "In Swedish,"

"Oh, come on!"

"No, if you're going to apologize, I want it right the first time." There's a hint of a smile and I know we're okay.

I brace my shoulders and begin in Swedish, "My apologies. I assumed the very worst and that was a mistake." I'm surprised how easy the words are to find again after so long dormant in my mind. He's waiting

36

patiently so I continue, "You were right, I was wrong, I'm sorry."

A huge grin breaks out across his face and I melt. "There, that wasn't so bad was it?" he says in perfect English. He leans past me to get the door and I catch a sniff of his wonderful aroma, "Come on, they'll wonder what we're doing out here."

We move into the back work room once again. Will and Holly are about to enact the same scenes that Ethan and Kate had just a few hours earlier when I realize I don't have my iPad. I jump up from my seat and say, "Sorry everybody, I've got to get my notebook. I'll be just a minute." I know right where I've left it, out on the kitchen table where I ate lunch with the others.

I hurry back down the hall, jump the little step into the living room, and round to the kitchen. It's just where I thought it would be. I grab it quickly and turn to rush back the way I had come. I scurry through the living room hastily, down the little step and there I lose my shoe. My heel slips and down I go.

The iPad falls from my hand. There's no catching myself. I brace for a hard landing. I fall awkwardly, hitting the sharp, rough metal edge of the bent threshold on the last stair. I feel flesh snag on the metal and muscle tear. Pain sears through my right forearm. My shoulder slams against the tile floor, knocking the wind out of me. I roll onto my back, wheezing for breath, grasping at my forearm. The pain is intense and the tears are instantly streaming.

Mentally, I check myself. I've fallen a hundred times, I know the rest of me is okay, but my arm isn't. I release my forearm just long enough to push myself up so that I'm leaning against the staircase bannister. I look at my hand, it's covered in blood. There's a growing pool of blood settling on the floor beneath my hanging arm. The metallic smell makes my stomach turn. I close my eyes and take a deep, calming (not really working) breath. I look at my forearm and its gushing blood. I press the wound to my chest to try to stop the flow. My white shirt quickly turns crimson, soaking up the blood.

From the quick look, I know it's a bad cut. It's about a four or five inch long jagged cut but the depth is what keeps replaying in my mind. I think I saw bone. I try not to faint at the possibility. How the hell did I manage this? I press my arm harder against my shirt and can feel the blood flowing through the shirt and into my bra. My skin beneath the shirt is feeling sticky. One great effort and I push myself to my feet. The pressure isn't enough; blood is trickling down my arm, dripping a trail at my feet. I leave the dead iPad on the floor and walk back to the others.

I must have startled Nicole because she starts screaming at me as soon as I walk through the door, "OH SHIT! Your arm...your shirt!" Really, I'm not worried about the shirt, I can replace it. Everyone seems on the cusp of panic, waiting for some break in me to react to. Holly goes for her cell phone and says she's calling 911.

I wave a bloody hand at her but stop when I see the blood I'm splattering on the floor. I press my arm harder into my shirt, "Don't call 911, that's only if you're dying." I am sure I'm not dying. I've had experience with that bitch, this doesn't feel the same.

Will crosses the room in three steps and grabs my arm. I howl in pain, the tears continue unremittingly as he takes a quick look and squeezes my t-shirt hem around it. "Come on," he demands and I follow since he's not letting go. He walks me back to the kitchen.

I yell over my shoulder to Nicole, "I'm so sorry, there's blood on your floor. If you get me a towel I can clean that up."

I'm ignored.

Will pulls me to the sink and starts the water. My arm is thrust under the current and I wince. "If you call me a cab I can get myself to a hospital," I say to the others who've followed us to the kitchen. I don't understand why everyone is ignoring me but paying attention to all of my blood.

"Hand me that dishtowel," Will asks of Holly. He stops the water but holds my arm over the sink. Good blood catcher. She passes the towel over immediately. He wraps the wound twice and squeezes it.

I snap at him, "That hurts!"

"It should, you need stitches." He holds the towel in place and says, "I know where the hospital is. I can take you." He looks at Todd and Nicole, "Can we postpone the audition?" There isn't any hesitation as they agree; my bloody mess has far surpassed their agenda. He nods in agreement and walks me out to his car. The beautiful Maserati, I hope I don't get blood in it.

Nicole runs up as Will opens the passenger door for me. "Your purse, you'll need your ID or something. I put your iPad in there too, but I think it's trashed. Sorry!" I thank her as Will pushes it down by my feet.

"Hold this tight," he says as if it's a commanding order. I have this insane need to say 'Yes Sir' but refrain. He looks pissed, brows furrowed, or maybe that's his overly concerned face.

He jogs around the car then hurries it out of the driveway. The Maserati speeds along the road and he insists that I'm not holding it tight enough.

"How do you know?" I ask, hoping not to faint from blood loss.

"My parents are doctors."

"Both of them?" I ask meekly. I am not worthy. I am not in his league.

"And my sister," he adds.

"Oh God," I whisper, realizing again my league has been blown out of the water.

"What?" He looks at me suddenly worried, "What? Are you going to faint, or something?" He makes several sharp turns and speeds through traffic.

"Listen, I'm not dying unless you wreck, slow down."

The car slows slightly but it's just for a turn and then another before he enters a parking lot. He parks near the emergency room at the hospital complex. "No arguing, you need stitches."

"Who's arguing?" I bitch back.

He looks me over, seeming to make mental notes then says, "You might even need a blood transfusion with the amount of blood you've lost. You're really pale, except for the freckles." I gape at him and he smiles crookedly. He's joking? Now? Shaking my head in disbelief I turn from him and manage to get my wallet out of my purse one handed - the less bloody hand - and unzip it. Blood trickles into the wallet and I curse.

He jumps from the car, jogging around it to my side. He kneels beside me and finishes taking out my insurance card then stuffs the wallet back into my purse leaving it on the floor of the car. He puts the grip-of-death again on the towel covering the wound and walks me into the ER.

The entrance of a Hollywood star and a bloody girl works like a charm. Willem is ushered almost immediately into a curtained off exam area and I'm graciously allowed to go with him. The women are ogling him, some of the men too. I simmer with jealousy then grasp that he's not really mine to be jealous about. Still, I am. I scoot up onto the exam bed and wait. Willem's passing the time by death-gripping the towel.

We're alone and I have time to breathe. It's only been about twenty minutes since I fell, that's pretty good time making it to the hospital in LA traffic. I glance around and my mind blurs with fear. One second I'm fine, the next I'm absorbed by terror. I lean forward and groan as I realize where I am and one of my biggest fears makes an appearance.

Willem releases my arm slightly and lays his free hand on my back, "You okay babe?" I shudder with fear. My body is trembling. A new wave of tears start. "Hey," he's leaning close, "the doctor will be here soon." I cry out and shake my head. He pushes my shoulders back until I'm lying down on the bed. "Shit, what's wrong?" He looks worried, fearful even. "Your eyes are dilated," his brows narrow, "you have no eye color!" He squeezes my arm tighter.

"I...I'm...afraid." My mind is rushing through memories at light speed. My teeth are chatting as if I'm in ice water. The pain, the screams are coming back and I'm reliving the viciousness of a long ago

42

moment. I shake my head trying to get the memories out. I grab for his t-shirt and beg, "Don't leave me, don't!" I gulp air but I can't breathe. "They never came for me!"

"I'm right here, baby girl." He leans over me, almost in a lying down hug, "Tell me what's wrong."

My free arm wraps around his neck and I hide my face in the base of his neck. Finally I inhale with a half laugh, "I'm terrified of hospitals, or doctors, I don't know exactly which."

He pulls back slightly to look into my fearful eyes, "Let's hope its hospitals or you'll never want to meet my family." I smile faintly at his joke and release him from my grasp.

A nurse pulls back the curtain and steps in with a smile. I just lay there semi-incapacitated with fear. Willem has a good hold on me, like an anchor for my sanity.

"Hi there, I'm Jen, your nurse." She walks to the side opposite Willem and says, "Let's have a look." She snaps on plastic gloves and takes my arm from Will. His hands wrap around my other arm and hand, our fingers interlace, keeping me safe. Jen removes the dishtowel and the blood flows again.

She pokes at it and I grunt in pain, then she sets my arm on the bed and turns to the metal cabinet behind her. She peeks through a couple of drawers then finds what's she's looking for. She comes back to the bed with something that looks like a giant feminine pad. She's grinning, "This will work." She looks at the towel with slight disgust, "I'm going to toss this." Will agrees. Jen takes a minute to wrap the wound with the giant padding. "I need to ask you some questions. Do you want your boyfriend to stay?"

I don't have time to clarify our relationship before he says, "I'm not leaving," sensing my rising panic.

She shrugs, "OK," as she drops the plastic gloves into the trash and picks up an iPad, "Your name," I calm slightly as my mind focuses on a task. She goes through the standard questions and I try to remain calm. "Any allergies?"

"Yes," I look at Will's smoky blue eyes for reassurance then turn to the nurse, "I'm allergic to eggs, and any egg based medicines. Sometimes I can eat them if they're baked, like in brownies," I'm rambling, must be the loss of blood or the near hysteria. "But not the good brownies, like the ones you get in Amsterdam, not that I have *any* experience with those." Will is openly laughing at me. "It's weird, I know." I look at him, yep; he's still laughing, and snap, "Shut up." He clears his throat and smiles, not hiding his amusement well.

Jen ignores half of what I've just said. "What happens?" she asks, jotting notes.

"I stop breathing. I carry an EpiPen in my purse."

She looks up, "OK, no eggs for you." She continues, "Date of your last period?"

"Do you really need to know that? I have a cut to my arm not my pussy," I snap.

"She lashes out verbally when she's in pain," Willem comments.

I gawk at him, "Fuck you."

"See what I mean?" he says to the nurse.

She remains impervious, "Yes, I need to know, when was it?"

I close my eyes, mortified to talk about my period in front of the beautiful man, "About two weeks ago."

She pats my bad arm, "Just a question I have to ask," and the doctor comes into the room.

I roll to my side as a wave of nausea hits me. He's young, attractive and one of the most frightening people I've ever seen. He takes a look at me and does away with his smile. He doesn't need to play the nice doctor with me. I try to crawl off of the bed and get to my feet. I want to leave, badly. Willem ends up pushing me back onto the bed.

He looks at the doctor, "She has a few issues with fear."

"Lucky me," he says for no one's benefit. I'm hyperventilating. My nails are digging into Will's arms but he doesn't notice. The doctor leans over me and says seriously, "The better patient you are, the faster I can get you out of here." He looks to the nurse and orders some medicine. I'll have to research it later, if I can even remember the name. I think my brain's short-circuiting.

"I'm going to touch your arm, Lauren. Is that alright?" I nod and shift as far away from him as I can get, leaving my arm behind. He touches it gently, removing the bloody pad. He moves my arm up over my head on the bed so the wound is flat and workable. He puts on plastic gloves and takes the little vial of liquid and a syringe from the nurse. "This is pain medicine, it's going to numb the area around your cut then I'm going to stitch your arm. Is this alright?" I nod and turn my head away. Will gently pushes my hair that's freed itself from my braid away from my face.

"I'm going to start now, Lauren," the doctor says. I look over quickly then back to Willem. I let out a slow breath of air through chattering teeth. "Don't hold your breath," he orders. He startles me with a touch and I take another difficult breath. Willem whispers in my ear that I'll be okay and I feel the prick of a needle. The tears start anew as the needle delves into my torn flesh several times. The doctor rubs my skin with a finger and asks if I can feel anything. Other than fear, I'm good.

"No," my voice is husky from crying, "I'm alright, you can start." I'm pleased that I can form a coherent sentence.

He sits on a wheelie-chair and pulls up a bright lamp. Willem is watching over me, protectively, and I release another haggard breath. He's watching the doctor work, turning to me occasionally to press little kisses on my forehead. "You're doing great." I nod hoping the stitching will be done soon. But it isn't, I've done a lot of damage to myself this time.

The snap of plastic brings me around from my mental fog. The tears have stopped but their dried tracks stain my face. Willem is still touching me gently, trying to keep me tethered to the world. "Go ahead and sit her up," the doctor says.

Willem pulls me up from the bed and I try to regain my equilibrium. "Sit for a minute, Lauren."

I nod and lift my arm to look. My skin has been washed orange and the stitches are hidden under a white bandage. There's a pinch in my shoulder and I look over to find another syringe. "This is for pain," he says, not really telling me. He's talking to Will, "This is pretty strong, so don't let her drive, operate heavy equipment," he smiles, "or be alone for a while."

"How many stitches did she get?" Will asks.

"The cut went down to the bone so most of the stitches are internal. Forty seven total. I put thirty inside."

"Does she need to come back to get the external ones removed?"

I am not a participant in this conversation, but still, it's interesting. I lean my head on Will's chest since he's so close. I feel his hand press against my hair, holding me close. Oooh, he smells wonderful and I inhale deeply.

"No, I used the dissolvable kind. She's good to go. Starting tomorrow she can have Advil for any pain." They shake hands. The nurse hands Will the iPad to sign then she leaves as soon as he's finished.

He stands in front of me and lifts me off of the bed. Once I'm steady on my feet he takes my hand in his and wraps an arm around me. I'm in the car before I know my feet are moving. I turn in the passenger seat and look at him as he gets into the car. He leans to me and presses a soft kiss to my lips, "You did good babe." I nod and curl up my legs. My eyes are closing as he asks, "Lauren, what hotel are you staying at? I don't know where to take you." I fade into a fuzzy gray.

Chapter 4

I feel myself move in the darkness but my body isn't working. I open my eyes and Willem is carrying me. This is nice. The world is gray, absorbed in shadows and unfamiliar but I'm not afraid. He stops for a moment to close a door with his foot. It only confirms my belief that he is the most graceful man in the world. I fade again.

The sound of his steps on a wooden floor wakes me slightly. I'm sitting up, sitting on something comfortable in the dark. He moves away quickly and a light comes on behind me, flooding the space with a warm white glow and long shadows. We must have been at the hospital for hours.

I look up and see I'm in a living room. White walls with lots of framed hanging pictures of people. Happy faces, they must be family. A large flat screen that's turned off sits across from me on a dark wooden stand. I can see the outline of my reflection in its obscurity. I'm a dark shadow of myself. I momentarily ponder where my demons have escaped to since my brain feels empty. My mind is noiseless. My focus shifts to books on a tall shelf to the left of the TV. I sit on the couch trying to concentrate on the titles to see if my books are there, but my eyes aren't quite working. I feel fuzzy, unfocused.

"Hi Mom," he says behind me in Swedish. I glance over my shoulder and see he's in the kitchen on his cell, "sorry, I know it's late, early, sorry. I need some advice." This is nice I think looking away from him; he's talking to his mom. "Medical." There a bit of silence while she talks. I can't hear what she's saying. "Lauren fell and cut her arm. Down to the bone."

More silence. He doesn't explain who Lauren is. My brain finally makes the connection from dinner; she already knows who I am. She likes my stories.

"She got forty seven stitches. The doctor said not to leave her alone. I brought her home. He gave her a really strong painkiller. She's really out of it, is that normal?"

I hiccup a laugh, is that normal? I repeat in my mind. Am I normal? I bleed like a normal person. I lift my arm and look at the bandage. I really am out of it.

"Oh, okay. What should I do?" She must really be giving him lots of great information or she could be telling him something that happened at home. "OK, Mom thanks. I love you."

He loves his mom. I feel a twinge of jealousy. Over his love or that he actually likes his mom enough to love her? I can't decide.

"Sorry I woke you." A bit more silence then he sets his cell on the kitchen counter. He squats in front of me and touches my face. He switches back to English for the benefit of my befuddled brain, "I have good medical advice." He smiles, "Mom says I have to take care of you."

"Okay," I think I'm fading again.

I blink my eyes open and am sitting again. This time I'm sitting on a blue and white abstract-patterned comforter. I focus on the pattern, it seems to be moving. I look away before it makes me nauseous and decide it must be the drugs. My pink painted toes are barely touching the hardwood floor. I fleetingly wonder where my shoes went to.

The walls are again white with three framed pictures of landscapes on a far wall. I concentrate on the pictures. Glacial mountains, a serene lake, and a castle that looks vaguely familiar. I know these places; I've even been to one of them. I went there on a school field trip. I'm gazing at the pictures when Willem returns.

He's carrying a basin and a few towels. He sets the dish on the nightstand by me and tosses the towels onto the bed. He leans a little closer to the lamp and switches it on. The room is bathed in soft light.

I'm watching him. I'm numb, even my brain is quiet.

"I like the drugs the doctor gave me," I say quietly. I'm not really sure I'm talking to him, "The voices in my head have gone. I'm really fucked up, you know."

He touches my hands, one in each of his. "You've mentioned that before. How many voices do you have in your head, Lauren?"

That's an interesting question, I count for a moment, "There's me and five others. Right now, it's just me, I think." I'm confused. "It's nice to be alone in my head." He nods agreeing but there's a grimace on his face.

He leans close and grabs me under the armpits, lifting me off the bed. I complain but it's really weak. I find my feet and stand, but I'm teetering. "Lauren," he explains, "I'm going to wash your clothes. I'll try to get the blood out, but no guarantees, okay?" I nod.

His agile fingers undo the button and zipper of my jeans. His hands slide under the material onto each side of my hips. His touch warms my skin. With gentle force he eases my jeans down. I place my hands on his shoulders as he lowers himself with my pants. He takes my left leg in his hand, "Lift your foot." I do and a leg of the jeans falls off. He repeats the process getting my right leg free. I look down as he looks up. My eyes blink heavily. I'm just grateful I wore pretty hip-huggers since he's at eye level with my panties. He stands and gently sets me back on the edge of his bed.

"I'd put you in the shower but I don't think you can do it alone."

Alone? I look into his beautiful eyes; does he want to shower with me?

He takes a washcloth from the bed and dunks it into the basin. A quick squeeze and the water falls back into the dish. He gently takes the wounded arm and turns it over. I gasp as he starts washing my arm. He looks at me, his eyes wide with anxiety, "Sorry, I got the water too hot, I guess." He washes the blood from my elbow, skipping the bandage then along each of my fingers. It feels like a warm, wet massage. I'm enjoying the drugs and his handiwork. He dunks the wet cloth again, rinsing it. Another squeeze and he takes my other arm. Up my arm...down along my hand, washing off the dried blood. Each of my fingers gets special treatment.

I have never felt so cared for.

He dunks the washcloth into the steaming water and rinses it again. His hand holds my neck and the cloth presses to my tear stains. I lean into the warm damp cloth and his hand. He wipes gently and the heat feels wonderful, comforting. The cloth softly wipes one cheek then another, one eyelid then another. He leans forward and presses a careful kiss to my lips.

"Lift your arms, Lauren." I do as told but my arms feel like weights. My t-shirt sticks to my skin where the tacky blood has started to dry. He peels it up over my head and drops it onto the jeans. The washcloth is rinsed again. A strong hand holds my shoulder, keeping me in place as he presses the cloth against my freckled skin. I watch his eyes; he's concentrating on his chore. Water from the cloth drips along my chest then my stomach as he moves it down my body. The cloth circles my stomach several times. "Lauren," my eyes find his again. He shakes his head and stands. He leans over me. I really don't know what he wants, a hug?

I feel a tug on my braid and he sets the band on the nightstand. His fingers untwine the braid, freeing the mass. He whispers, "There's no blood in your hair." I sit silently in a drug induced fog.

Willem squats in front of me again. His arms are around my back then my breasts lower slightly as he pulls my bra forward and off my shoulders. Normally I'd be embarrassed but I'm not. My vanity and humility must be taking a drug break.

I'm not expecting this either, I want him. I want to lean forward to touch his chest. I want to bring him close to me and fold my arms around his neck. I ache to reach out and touch him. I want to caress his face and run my fingers through his soft dirty blonde hair but I don't.

He adds the bra to the pile of clothes on the floor. Taking up the wet cloth, he drags it heavily across my chest. I inhale as his fingers linger along my breast. The cloth finds the fold of my breast and he wipes beneath it. My breath is heavy and I'm panting slightly. The wet cloth moves up over my nipple. My eyes focus on his face but his eyes won't meet mine. He's concentrating on his task. I just need to lean

54

forward but I'm having trouble focusing. The cloth moves to my other breast and it's caressed and cleaned as well.

He leans back and places the washcloth in the basin. He takes up the dry towel beside me and pats dry my chest and stomach. Dropping it to the laundry pile he stands up. A swift move and he steps away from me. I close my eyes trying to calm the inferno he's created.

He's standing in front of me when I open my eyes. He shakes open a white V-neck undershirt and drapes it over my head, taking care with each of my arms as he slides them through his shirt. Leaning close he wraps his arms around my chest and lifts me from the bed. I'm leaning against him as he grabs the comforter and tosses it aside. He sets me back on the bed. "Sleep now baby girl. I'll make sure you're safe." I believe all of his words as I lay my head on his pillow. I feel the comforter fold over me and I close my eyes.

Tears trickle from my eyes, landing on his pillow as sleep overcomes me.

I have never felt so cared for.

From my sleep I hear a phone ring. It echoes through the silence. Willem answers it with a quick hello. "Hey Nicole," he says. "Yeah, she's good. We were at the hospital for a while." There's silence and the fog of sleep retakes me momentarily. I hear him speak; his voice is husky and masculine and stirs something deep inside of me, "Forty seven stitches. Can we give her a day?" There's silence as Nicole talks then he says, "Really? The Late Show? What time? Okay, I'll get her there. She's staying with me. The doctor gave her some fucked up medicine." He laughs, "Yeah, I'll be good. I'm sleeping on the couch. Night Nicole."

I grimace and reach for my shoulder. I ache all over and roll onto to my back. I blink my eyes open. The light of a television illuminates the shadowy bedroom. I stare at the TV for a moment and see it's a program about motorcycles. I look beside me and find Willem watching the flat screen. He's propped up on some pillows, very relaxed. He's wearing plaid flannel pajama pants and a white t-shirt that's identical to the one I'm wearing.

I push the comforter aside and roll towards him. My bare leg is lying over the comforter and I hug the fluffy blanket. My movement catches his attention and he looks down at me. "Sorry, did the TV wake you?" he asks.

I shake my head no. "Is it very late?"

He looks to his nightstand and turns back to me, "No, it's almost eleven." He slides down the pillows and settles beside me, "Are you feeling any better?"

"My shoulder hurts. I feel like I hit something really hard," I smile. Funny in my own mind. I stretch

56

out my wounded arm and lay it on his chest. He smiles for me.

He shifts again so we're lying closer, eye to eye, heart to heart. "Can I ask you something?" he asks and I nod. "You said at the hospital that they left you? Who did you mean?"

"My parents," my voice is very low. "I'm sorry. I shouldn't have bothered you with that."

"It's not a bother."

"My parents are dead now. It's all in the past."

"So, they won't mind you talking about them. Come on, Lauren, tell me."

I take a deep breath. I haven't talked about any of this before. I shrug and grimace at the movement. He reaches across the space between us and rubs my shoulder. After a moment his hand moves from my shoulder to my back and lays there. I look into his eyes and am reassured by the kindness I see.

"I was nine when we moved to Stockholm. My parents were retired. They wanted to see the world. They bought a nice apartment, in a good part of town. I was ten when they left me for the first time. Just a few days to Copenhagen. A few days here and there to Paris. The few days became a few weeks to Russia, Italy." His eyes are so beautiful, smoky blue and kind. "I was twelve when they left me. I was alright. I could take care of myself. There was always money on the credit card Dad gave me. I'd stop on my way home from school and pick up food from the grocery store or a restaurant. I knew to keep the doors locked." I shrug and instantly regret the movement.

"How come no one noticed? The authorities should have stepped in and been your guardian, if your parents didn't want to," he says quietly.

"I was never late to school, never missed a day. I was a good student so there was never any need for a teacher conference." I stop for a moment trying to decide how much to share. Finally my eyes meet his; I've made a decision while the voices have disappeared. I find a little courage. "My neighbor noticed. She knew my parents were gone. Mrs. Persson, she was very nice. She'd invite me for holiday dinners. She became like a mother to me. She warned me about boys," I wink at him and smile at the memories. He returns my smile warmly. "She had a daughter my age so we became good friends. Malin was her name."

"Was?"

I scoot closer to him and he wraps his arms around me. I lean my head on his chest, drape my wounded arm over his stomach. "Is this okay?" I ask. He reaches to the nightstand for the remote and turns off the TV. He settles himself in the darkness, keeping me in his arms. I whisper, "Malin was killed when she was seventeen."

"I'm sorry," he says. He places a kiss on my forehead, "Don't think about it tonight, beautiful. You need to rest." I push the memories of Malin aside for the moment. I curl up next to Willem and feel safe in his arms. It has taken only twenty-eight years to feel this way.

Chapter 5

I'm woken by a gorgeous man sitting on my side of the bed. He's carrying a tray and I peek over its edge to see food and a drink. I wiggle to sitting up and wipe the sleep from my eyes.

"Breakfast in bed, beautiful," he says with a smile. I'll need to thank his mother for teaching him to go all out on the taking care of me advice. "I hope you like bagels."

I'm looking at a meal: a bagel with cream cheese, colorful fruit and some OJ. "This looks great," I say returning his smile. I sit up more and he passes over the tray.

"I did the laundry while you were sleeping last night."

"How are my jeans?" Shirt be damned. I just want my jeans to be okay.

"They're fine. The stain on your shirt and bra didn't come out. I tossed 'em, hope that was okay." I nod and spread cream cheese over the bagel. A big mouthful. I didn't realize I was so hungry. "I hope it's okay, I got your hotel room card from your purse. I'm going over by the hotel so I thought I'd stop and get you some more clothes. Nicole said you have an interview later."

"Yeah," I swallow hard, not wanting to talk with my mouth full. "I have to go on the Late Show. It's been set up for a while. I need to get to the auditions too."

"Those have been postponed until tomorrow. Nicole's going to give you a day to recoup." He smiles again, "Probably takes time to get that much blood off the floor."

"You know what people say," he looks to me, almost innocently, "Everyone loves a piece of ass, just not a smart one." I give him a nasty look but it's forgotten as his smile lights up and he laughs. I take another bite and ask, "Can you get my burgundy dress? It's hanging in the closet area. Room 513. Oh, I need my shoes too."

He leans forward and presses a kiss to my lips, cream cheese and all, "I'll call you if I can't figure out which shoes go with which dress."

I watch him walk out the bedroom door admiring the view and hear the garage door close. He could kiss me every day for a thousand years and I still couldn't get enough of him.

I'm lazy in bed for a long time. Rolling to his side of the bed I hug his pillow and inhale his smell. I scoot a little further onto his side and begin exploring. Pulling open his nightstand drawer I poke through what's not mine to look at.

The contents range from boring to interesting. A couple of pens, a scratch pad for late night phone call notes. A paperback book about rampaging dinosaurs. A box of condoms. Man-whore! I hold it up to examine the box, it's new and unopened. I set them back and close the drawer.

I get my lazy ass out of bed and find my jeans lying on his dresser, folded. Jeez, what kind of man folds laundry? I have no practical experience with men so I blow it off, maybe all men fold laundry. I step into my jeans and scoot them up over my butt. I leave on his t-shirt since mine has been irreparably damaged by the blood. I gather up my tray and dishes and leave the bedroom for some more exploring.

At the far end of the hall are a small set of stairs down into a big room. It has many ceiling to floor windows that are looking out onto a breathtaking view of mountains. It strikes me as odd that I don't even know where in Southern California I actually am. The drug the doctor gave me must have been really strong to wipe away any memories of getting to his house.

One side of the room must be the playroom, with a pool table, leather couch and a large flat screen. An Xbox sits on the floor before it, several controllers haphazardly lying on the hardwood floor. The other side has a weight set and a treadmill. I run my hand over the weights, knowing I couldn't pick them up.

From the big room I return to the hall and open doors as I walk back towards the kitchen. Two smaller bedrooms, a common bathroom. Back in the kitchen I set my plate and glass in the sink and wash them. I set those next to the tray on the counter to dry. I don't want to be a bad house guest. In memoriam to MTV Cribs I open his fridge finding lots of fruits and veggies. I pick up a brown bottle of beer and read a European label. A bottle of white wine sits in the holder on one side of the split metal doors. I close the door and continue my wandering.

I end up in front of his pictures. All of the happy faces captured in time. There are so many people, so many faces and expressions. I mentally run through all the people I know. Sadly, I don't know this many people.

I step away from the happy people and work my way to the book shelf. This is more my territory. Leaning slightly to read the titles easier I trace my fingers over the covers. Some paperbacks...some hardbacks but none are mine. I'll have to get him a set.

On one shelf I find old scripts. They're bound individually so they look almost like books without the stylized covers. I pull one out and find it a little worn. There are scribbles on the front page. Signatures I assumed. Flipping through it I find occasional jotted notes on different pages. This might be valuable so I put it back carefully.

Walking back to his bedroom I open the closet door searching for fashionable entertainment. Flicking a switch, the small room is illuminated. There's a rack of shoes and I step close. I pick up a pair of dress shoes and turn them over examining the crafted leather.

They're big and weighty, well crafted, and expensive. I set them back and pick up another pair. These are well broken in; the dark leather is supple and soft. I set those back and continuing exploring. Another shelf of more casual shoes, athletic ones. There's a row of suits, shades of grays, blacks, navy blues. Crisp, linen dress shirts in colors that coordinate to the suits. There's an assortment of ties in a variety of colors and patterns. I like his color choices. It proves to me that he's not just vanilla and bagels.

I run my fingers over his everyday hanging clothes and close the closet door behind me. I flip the light switch turning it off and return to the big bed. Tired from my exploration I crawl into his side and hug his pillow. I fall asleep to his fragrance, warm and comfortable in the knowledge that this man has no secrets. The last thing I think before I drift off is to wonder what kind of man, raised in a secure, happy family, has no secrets?

"Thank you for getting my interview clothes for me," I say. He's gone by the hotel earlier in the morning, shortly after the sun had come up and well before I wanted to get out of bed. I didn't mention my exploration when he returned and woke me from my slumber.

He's standing behind me, which is no problem since I'm so short and can't possibly block his line of sight. "OK, tell me about all these people." I'm in

64

front of the mass of pictures and want to put names and relations to faces.

"Are you sure?" he whispers in my ear sending shivers along my spine. "There're a lot of people in there."

I glance over my shoulder, finding his bright eyes on me, "Only if you want to."

He smiles, I melt, then he starts by pointing to a large group portrait, "Left to right, OK? These are my grandparents, my dad's parents." They are gray haired, but you can tell they are still in love, holding hands as they stand next to, his finger moves to the next person, "That's my dad, Oscar. My mom, Klara." I lean in for a better look. His parents are attractive, both with soft shades of blonde-gray hair. He starts jumping around, "I'll go oldest to youngest for kids to save on confusion. This is me. I'm sure you guessed." He seems to be the tallest of the group. He's insanely handsome amongst a group of insanely handsome people.

"When was this taken?" I ask engrossed in the faces and names he's providing.

He thinks for a moment, "This was two years ago, summer, my birthday actually. This was taken at my parents' summer house." He smiles shyly then refocuses, "This is my sister Rhea. She's the family doctor I told you about. She's single and a constant disappointment to my parents." I smile at his amusement. She's lovely; a tall, pretty blonde. A younger version of her mother. "This is my brother Lucas. He's an architect in Stockholm, that's his wife standing beside him. She was pregnant at the time." I can see the beginning bulge of her belly as they stand close together. Lucas' hand rests on the swell. "They have a boy. He's a year and half old now."

"So you're an uncle?"

He smiles warmly, "Yes, many times over. My big family keeps getting bigger." He points to another, "This is my other brother, Elias." He stands out in the crowd with brown hair. A dirty-blonde haired woman stands next to him; several children are sitting on the ground at their feet. "I'm afraid he's another doctor but a psychiatrist. Rhea gives him shit about that, about not being a real doctor. He's married, that's his wife. They have four children. I think they started having babies the second they met each other. Three boys and a girl, all under the age of nine. You can see them all here in the picture."

"He doesn't look like the rest. Dark hair...dark eyes."

"We used to tell him that Mom and Dad picked him up off the side of the road when he was a baby." He smirks, "His kids are taking after him." Little brown haired children pictured sitting on the green summer grass. He smiles crookedly, "The last of my siblings," he points to two beautiful young women, they could be twins. "There's Lili, she's a college student in England and Astrid. She's in school still, living with my parents. The lady with her arm around Astrid is my grandmother, ah, my mom's mom."

"How old are Lili and Astrid, they're beautiful."

"Lili actually models part-time for college money. She's twenty four. She's graduating this coming spring. She's getting her degree in biology."

"Let me guess, another doctor?"

"Sort of, she wants to be a researcher. She'll go to med school and then make a decision about what she wants to do. Last time we talked she said something about genetics."

"Smart and pretty."

He nods and agrees, "Astrid is eighteen. She'll graduate in the spring too. Guess I better book my plane ticket for home. The girls are graduating. It's a big family," he says as his finger drops from the picture.

"You all get along? You like each other?" I ask incredulously, as if the idea is preposterous.

He smiles, "Yeah, especially now that I don't live at home with them."

I'm studying the chess board with great determination. I might be horrible at "Whack-a-Mole" but I'm great at chess. I usually play against the computer so I have to adjust to an old-fashioned board and a human opponent. Willem and I are sitting at the far end of his kitchen. He's set the game out on the small kitchen table and we're being playful adversaries.

He's just as good as I am, making me think about every move. He's playing dirty, unfairly using his good looks and charm to sidetrack me.

"I know what you're doing. You're trying to distract me," I say to him when he tells me he's hot and removes his shirt. I'm taken aback by his desire to win at any cost. "It won't work. I did research on you before I came to California." I move my queen.

"Really?" He leans over the board, his muscles flexing in the warm sunlight that bathes the kitchen from another ceiling to floor window (which actually is distracting), "Did you find out anything interesting?" he asks.

He's still studying the board when I reply, "I know you're a man-whore." He looks up and I beam at him. "Oh, yes, the internet is full of sensational stuff about you and all the women you've dated and been with."

His eyes fall to the chessboard. He's not smiling anymore, "Don't believe all the crap you find online." He moves his rook and looks up, "I'm not a man-whore."

"Yes you are."

"No, I'm not." He laughs, "I would know if I am."

"I found numerous articles about you and different women in different countries."

"Lauren," he says my name as if he's scolding me, "I was in a serious relationship up until two years ago. We were together for almost four years."

"Yeah," the producer ex-girlfriend. I have a ridiculous need to refer to her as The Bitch. I only read articles saying their relationship ended. Nothing discovered on who dumped who, "after that."

"Having my picture taken with a woman I'm talking to doesn't mean I'm fucking her. It means I was talking with her. I hate the fucking paparazzi."

I make a decision about a chess piece and something more serious. I place my fingers on the queen, and swallow hard, "You know if you Google me you'll find all the normal stuff. Generic, fluffy biography stuff, info on my books." I stop and look up at him; my voice is deadly calm, "If you Google Malin Persson," I look unwavering into the beautiful eyes, "you'll find out something no one knows. I will be the one the articles refer to as fellow teen or friend." My eyes leave his and sadness overwhelms me, "Queen takes the knight, checkmate." The queen fells the king. I find his eyes, "Please don't think the worst of me." I get up and walk away from the table.

I'm standing in the shower, water rushing over me. I've trashed the bandage, letting the water have free access to my wound. It stings a bit but I've felt worse pain. Behind me the shower door slides open then closes. I open my eyes as he wraps his arms around me. My back presses to his chest, his muscular arms enveloping me. The warmth of his body radiates through me. My heart beat spikes with adrenaline. The pressure against my backside tells me he's happy to see me. I step forward letting the water rush over him and turn in his arms. My fearful eyes find his. "Did you Google me?" I ask timidly, afraid of the answer.

"No, I don't want to know anything about you that you won't tell me yourself."

"OK," I agree but I know that he'll have to find out sometime. I stretch up on my toes. My breasts drag up his chest, nipples perking as the water caresses our skin before it falls to the shower floor. I press a bold kiss to his lips. His hands push the wet mass of hair from my face then pull me to him for another fervent kiss. This one, like the one in the car, is overwhelming. I'm consumed into the moment, into his passion and hunger. His hands glide over my wet body learning my curves intimately. He presses me back against the cool tile wall and leans down, finding my mouth with his. He's demanding, passionate with his caresses. His lips press along my neck which immediately sends my hoochie into overdrive. I gasp as his lips find my breast. My hands hold his head close as he plucks the rosy peak with his tongue then his teeth. A shudder of pleasure runs throughout my body.

Katherine McLellan

My lips find his again as he bends to pick me up. My arms twine around his neck and shoulders. My legs wrap around his lean waist as he presses me against the shower wall. My lips are swollen with desire, the salty taste of his skin on my tongue. He's waiting for me, searching my eyes for unspoken permission. "I don't know what I'm doing," I say nervously.

He reaches past me and turns the water off. "I do," he says confidently, carrying me out of the shower and back into the bedroom.

He's sitting on the edge of the bed with me straddling him. I'm sitting on his long athletic legs, my hands trailing slowly along his stomach muscles. The house is quiet, not interrupting our intimacy. His fingers are intertwined in the wet mass of my hair. Like a soaked sponge it's dripping water endlessly over the both of us. His lips are pressing against mine, caressing me. His tongue darts in and out, exploring my mouth. I'm dazed with passion. My fingers glide south along his stomach. A moan escapes his lips as I touch his manhood. I run my hand along his shaft. He's so hard but the skin is so soft, it's almost like velvet.

"Are you on the pill or something else?" he asks breathlessly through kisses.

"Something else," I murmur returning my attention to his lips.

"What do you want, Lauren?" he asks, his voice husky with desire.

I want everything from him. "I want you to stop talking," I smile through my kisses. My hands move up along his stomach, over his powerful chest, "I don't know how," I plead. My eyes search his, "I want to feel loved," finally answering his question. He rolls over onto the bed taking me with him. His weight is more than I expect and my legs open as an invitation.

He props himself up on an arm and leans slightly from me, "Are you sure?" I nod. I've never been surer of anything. I want him. He leans down and presses a kiss to my lips. My body thrills with excitement. His hand massages my breast then traces my sensitive skin along my stomach with his fingertips. Those smoky blue eyes of his search my damaged soul. His fingers run along my hips then he shifts and takes my backside within his hand.

I love everything about him. The way his back feels beneath my fingers, the pressure of his weight on me. He's kissing me, his eyes close momentarily in pleasure. His erection, rock hard against my leg presses forward and enters me slowly taking measure of every inch of my body. I cry out and pull him tighter to me. He stops and looks at me, those beautiful eyes searching for an answer to an unspoken question.

"Don't stop," I beg in a whisper, "please." He moves again, boldly. His strong thrusts become paced and pleasurable. My body is caressed again and again.

I can only concentrate on one thing, his rhythmic movements. My hand slides along his toned back down to his ass. The muscles are flexing, moving, enticing me forward. His aroma intoxicates my mind. His breath is caught on my lips. We find a rhythm working for our shared pleasure. The intensity has swallowed me whole. I am on the brink of a precipice. I only want more. I shout as my release comes, arching my back, pressing my hips against his, wanting him, wanting him inside me. He finds his release too, calling my name.

Tears trickle from my eyes and I beam as he looks me over. "Why the tears?" he asks quietly. "Was I that bad?" he adds jokingly.

I giggle and lean forward pressing a kiss to every inch of skin I can reach, "No, you…are…wonder…ful!" I'm trying to catch my breath. I'm grinning stupidly, so elated and happy. "I thought they broke me. All these years I was so sure." He's looking at me like I'm a bit crazy, "I mean, I know they broke me mentally and I just figured they broke that part of my body too."

"Who? Your parents?"

"No," I shake my head. I don't want to tell him. Not him, when he's become so precious to me.

"The stuff on Google?"

I nod. A wave of concern washes over his face. I lean forward and press a long, inviting kiss to his lips.

"I want you to do that to me again." His crooked smile radiates back.

For hours Willem does nothing but worship my body. I'm beginning to think he's a sex god among men. His skill is incredible. Every time he takes me to a new height of ecstasy before my passion is released.

He lies with his head on my chest. His skin against mine. The way we are meant to be. His fingers trail along my satisfied and sensitive skin. "I want to kiss every freckle," he says.

"Hmm," I murmur in pleasure, "that could take days, weeks possibly."

"Years even, it's quite a lofty task." I sputter out a snide but uncommitted reply. "We need to get going. You have a date with a comedian."

I lazily look at the clock on his nightstand and realize the day has drifted by in the arms of his love. I sit up and run my fingers through his dirty blonde hair just as I have wanted to since we met and realize disappointingly, "It's too late to do my hair."

"I think your hair is beautiful."

I smile, my heart warmed by the unexpected compliment, "Ringlets it is."

I'm standing behind a heavy burgundy curtain at the edge of backstage and my hands are shaking. Willem is beside me telling me that everything will be alright. Part of me wants to believe him. Things have

74

changed and I don't handle change well. I intertwine my hands together and sadly recognize the fact that my wrap dress is the same color as the stage curtain. Behind it, out near the audience the host, Rob Wheeler, is going through the second half of his comedy routine. He's warming up the crowd for my arrival with his easy smile and quick wit. I tell myself just to walk carefully away from the curtain opening as quickly as I can. This way the colors are separated, me from the curtain.

It was only twenty minutes ago, well after Will and I had arrived that the producer told me the interview subject was being changed. They didn't want to talk about the book to movie or the new book next year. She holds out an eight by ten picture of Willem walking me into the hospital from the day before. My sense of time is off-balance. It feels like I've known him longer. I look at the picture again. Our first picture together. I internally giggle like a schoolgirl. The paparazzi have been spending their money on long lens. It's not a great shot but it's a close up of him and me walking through the parking lot, my arm pre-stitches and bloody covered in the towel. He and I, together with blood are so much more interesting. Nicole's words of 'No such thing as bad publicity' come to mind.

Willem is whispering in my ear, but not touching me. We're in public and they'll be no pictures of us canoodling. "I'll wait in the green room. You'll do fine. Just concentrate on what he's talking to you about. You'll be great! It's only five minutes."

Five minutes of living Hell. I am the last of three guests. The two other guests, a politician and a music mogul along with the musical number and a comedy routine that involves dogs have eaten up most of the show's time. I will only be with Rob, on stage, in front of the crowd and the world for five minutes. I hope I don't throw up.

Last guest up and ready, that's me. I'm standing next to the producer. She has her hand on my non-wounded arm, ready to release me onto the stage at the precise moment. We're back from the break. The commercials will be filled in later when the show airs.

Rob is on the other side of the curtain and I hear him say, "Our last guest tonight is Lauren Radford, award winning novelist who has set Hollywood on fire," Have I? Really, on fire? "Her books have sold more than two hundred million copies worldwide. Please give a big welcome..."

The curtain opens four feet and the producer almost shoves me out. I plaster a big smile to my face and stand straight. I walk carefully past the curtain and immediately to Rob. He's smiling too, all happy to see me. This is sort of an interview coup for him. I don't do interviews or at least, not often.

He takes my hand and places a gentle kiss to my cheek. I turn to the audience and give a little wave

as I step up onto the platform that holds his desk (I
don't know why a comedian needs a desk) and the
three guest chairs. The two other guests stand and
give me a quick welcome. My burgundy dress hangs
nicely on my curves Willem told me, giving me a much
needed confidence boost. My ringlets are
uncontrollable and I have managed not to fall yet. So
far, so good.

Rob takes his seat behind the desk as I take the
guest chair closest to him. "Lauren, welcome to the
show. It's your first time with us."

I smile, "Yes, I'm very excited to be here. Thank
you for inviting me."

"First time in LA too?" I nod and agree. "Now I
heard that you got hurt yesterday, is that true?"

"I did," my smile is lost but not far away, "My
book, *Stockholm to DC*, is being made into a movie. I
was at the auditions for the actors and fell." There is a
unanimous sympathetic groan from the audience.

"I have a picture," he holds up the picture the
producer has already shown me. He's pointing for the
audience's benefit, "This is a very bloody you," I agree,
"and who's this?" Everyone knows who he's pointing
to, Will is not unknown, but I answer his question for
the half a percent of the world's population who've
been sheltered from knowledge of this beautiful man.

"That's Willem Rysberg, the actor from
Sweden. He was auditioning for the lead in the movie
when I fell."

"Very handsome guy."

"Yes, he is." No reason to deny the truth. "He's also handy to have around when there's an emergency."

"How so?"

"Well, he stepped up to help when I fell. He cleaned the wound and took me to the hospital for stitches. I couldn't ask for more than that."

"Sounds like a good guy."

I smile, "Yes, he's a credit to his Viking heritage and the good name of Rysberg." There's a laugh from the audience.

Rob smiles charmingly, "So, can we see your stitches?"

I return his smile; "Sure," I hold my arm up so he, and everyone, can see the stitches. I'm sure the camera is zooming in for a close up of them. There's a communal groan from the audience. I'm pointing out the stitches, "I have a total of forty seven stitches but most of them are inside." I look up from the wound and see Rob is eating this up so I add, "The cut went down to the bone. It's really a unique experience to see your own bones; of course, there's a lot of blood involved to accomplish that."

"Well," he leans back, "that's quite the fall you had. Your fans will start covering you in bubble-wrap." A collective laugh.

"There won't be any permanent damage, just a scar, so I'll keep writing."

"Now, I hear that you have a new book coming out next year. Why don't you tell us about it?"

"It's called *The Gray Work* and you are going to love it!" I smile and give a brief synopsis of my new book. It's a Heaven versus Hell thriller. The more I think about it the more I like Cole for the main character of that story. I put the thought aside and field questions that Rob throws at me. I see the large clock on the wall near the audience is counting down. I've almost finished.

"Lauren, thank you for coming to see us tonight! Her book comes out in March everyone. I'm sure it will be another smash! Thank you." He stretches out his hand for mine, giving it a light squeeze. I wave to the audience as he continues, "Tomorrow night folks we'll be joined by Chef Jack Thompson." He starts listing guests so I tune out for a moment, "see you then!" I sit and wait for the light on the camera to dim. That's my 'OK to Move' light. Once it goes out I get up and shake Rob's hand again. I say my goodbyes to the other guests and try to step off the little stage gracefully. I work my way past the curtain and find Willem backstage waiting for me.

"Was I okay?" I ask before he says anything.

"A credit to my Viking heritage?" He's dazzlingly beautiful, completely amused. People are starting to take notice of us. "The good name of Rysberg?" He turns with me as we fall in step, laughing at my comments, "My parents are going to love that."

Chapter 6

I pop a French fry in my mouth and grin with delight. "You've never been on a show like that?" I ask, curious about everything involving Willem. We're sitting at a small burger restaurant a few miles from the studio. Fries cannot satisfy the kind of hunger I'm feeling. The food is decent but the place is nearly empty of patrons. It looks as if it's stuck in a time warp, the seventies, sadly, with baby-puke green plastic seats and laminate tables.

Will shakes his head no, "I really haven't. The roles I've played have been small and varied. Lots of independent films. No big blockbuster where the studio wants me out on the late night circuit." He takes one of my fries. "Was Rob right, about your books? You've sold that many?"

"Yes," I'm leaning in wanting to lick the French fry salt from his lips but resist. "The books are popular. I like that they're available electronically, saves trees." I shrug, "I love what I do." I swallow a fry and ask, "Why acting? It sounds like your family is more about medicine than acting?"

"It's what I do. I love acting," he smiles warmly and I melt into a ball of goo. "My parents recognized my creativity when I was young, which basically means I ran around the house dressed as superheroes." I laugh at the image of young Willem impersonating

Batman. "They encouraged the arts but probably thought it would end up being a good hobby or something for me, not my career. I never wanted to be just a doctor or just a mechanic or soldier. When I act I'm able to become many different people. I travel, meet new people. I've seen a lot of the world because of the roles and movies I've been in," he pauses for a moment, "I always appreciate that I am a working actor. I could live in this town and not be hired for any roles. It's a lucky combination of things that I get to do what I love and make a good living." He splits the last fry in half, one for me and one for him. "Besides, I have siblings so that my parents don't get disappointed in me," he smiles again, joking.

"What kind of medicine does your family practice?"

His voice is strong and masculine, I love listening to him talk. "My dad is an obstetrician, a baby doctor."

"Did he deliver you?"

His smile meets his striking eyes, "No, a friend of his did. But he did deliver my two youngest sisters."

"I can't imagine what it's like to grow up in a big family," I say absentmindedly.

"There's no privacy," he answers, "*And*," he says exaggeratedly, "Mom is an eye surgeon." I look at him inquisitively, "She puts eyes back together if they've been injured." I breathe a 'Wow' as he continues, "My sister is general practice. You know, a little bit of everything like a family doctor. She has her own office near Gamla Stan. She sees a lot of tourists." I nod, knowing the beautiful old-town area of Stockholm he's talking about.

"Your family is full of overachievers."

He agrees, "All of us Rysbergs are held to high standards. What did your parents do, before they retired?" He doesn't add 'and abandoned you' but I know that's what he's thinking.

"My dad worked for a computer company. He retired a VP," he looks at me blankly so I clarify, "Vice President, East Coast division. He had stock options and a great retirement package." Good for him. I cannot remember my father working any day of my life. "My mom didn't work when my brothers were young but she worked part time before I was born and Dad retired. I think she said it was at a clothing store."

"Where did you go to college?" he asks.

I smile, he makes me feel very smiley. "I went to Cornell University for my bachelors."

"In what?"

"Literature, of course." As if there would be any doubt in my choice of majors. "How about you? Did you go to college?"

He nods and pushes the empty fry plate from in between us. Now it's just him and me and the foot of space that separates us. "My parents were very serious about that. I went to Stockholm University and got my humanities degree. After that I went to New

York and started acting. I was lucky to find roles. I just want to do something significant now."

"I understand, you want to make an impact."

He's unabashed, "I want to be the one the studios call first."

My fingers trace a pattern along the back of his hand. We cannot touch in public, ground rules have been set but he's not pulling his hand away. "Can I ask something?" I feel a little awkward and shy, "Can I stay with you tonight?"

He smiles, "I expect you to stay with me until you leave for New York. I want to spend every minute with you." I return his smile.

I close the garage door and step further into his kitchen. His house is a house, not a small mansion like Nicole's. One story, but spacious with great views during the daylight of the distant mountains out tall windows. It feels comfortable and homey. I walk along the hall towards his bedroom following Willem, needing to change for the night. He turns on his heel suddenly and takes me in his arms. His lips are hard against mine. I collapse to the hardwood floor and he follows me.

"I want you now," he growls and my hoochie wakes up instantly. "I've wanted you all night," he says between kissing me and pushing my dress aside revealing my bra and panties. He pushes down my lacy bra cup and my breast is bare to his assault. His tongue plays with my nipple, sucking and kissing. My body flushes and burns with sudden rapture as a moan escapes my lips.

I fumble with his pants before he pushes my hands aside, unzipping them himself. His erection is free and he rips my panties from my body. My body rushes with excitement. I really didn't want to wear them again anyway. He shifts his hips and enters me with a hurried thrust. I grab at his arms, his back, any part of him that can keep me tied to his passion.

"You're so wet," he breathes, continuing his savagery. I'm being pounded into the hardwood floor and I love it. My hand finds his backside and I pull him hard, further into me. His hand grabs my breast and massages it. My nipple shrieks in pain as he rubs it hard. "Come for me, come on!" I'm breathing hard, the passion is unrelenting. I want him. I want him hard and fast. I realize I need him, with a twinge of anxiety. His mouth replaces his fingers and nips my breast with his teeth and I shout out, coming hard. My high-heeled legs wrap around his waist as aftershocks rake over my body and he comes with a groan.

He lays on me; his hand rests on my breast. His rapid breathing is in my ear as he asks, "It wasn't too rough, was it?" I can hardly form a sentence but words of pleasure and adoration are expressed. He really is a sex god.

I throw him a fake nasty look and admonish, "You trashed my underwear. I might have wanted to wear those again but now I can't."

"I'll buy you some more." He's laughing at me and I love it.

"Fine," I'm pawing through the small overnight bag he brought back from the hotel looking for some clothes, "you can tear any of my clothes you want as long as I wearing them." I smile, and blush, it's this damn afterglow. Or is it love? Ah, crap, I realize I'm in love with him. I'm in love with Willem Rysberg. I lose my smile. That's really fucked up. How can I be in love with him, we've only known each other for a few days. I live on the other side of the country. Not to mention all of my psychological issues, the voice inside my head kindly reminds me.

"What's wrong?" he asks. Fuck, he's in tune with my mood swings.

"Nothing," I'll be the stupidest person in the world if I tell him how I feel. No, not going to do that. Instead I take my personal little bag to the bathroom and shut the door. I'm an idiot.

I'm wearing his t-shirt again and fresh panties when I leave the bathroom. He's watching me move around his bedroom, waiting for me. Patiently.

With a giggle I hop onto bed beside him and grin like I'm the cat who's eaten the canary. "What do you want to do now?" I ask innocently, batting my eyelashes. *Please say sex...please say sex.*

"You don't seem to know much about sex Lauren." Is he asking me or telling me? A grin emerges across his face. "I thought we'd try something new for you. If you've done this before you'll tell me, OK?"

"Yes Sir," I say with a firm voice. I resist the urge to salute.

His smile matches mine as he lies back on the bed and quickly removes his flannel pajama pants, tossing them aside to the floor. I'm just sitting there, my mouth slightly agape. He's naked and beautiful and he's mine, sort of. His muscles are so well defined along his arms and stomach and I swallow hard. His eyes are twinkling with mischief as his hand falls to my thigh. He's enjoying me, enjoying the view. There's a lot to take in as my eyes wander freely over his toned body.

His hand moves from my thigh to the t-shirt and he sits up to take it off. "Unless you want me to tear those off," he's eyeing my new panties. I sit up on my knees and wiggle out of them, tossing them to the floor beside the bed. I'm as naked as he is, just not as attractive. The freckles hide my flush. His hands find mine and our fingers intertwine.

"Come here beautiful," he says and I dissolve into gooeyness. He moves me so that I'm straddling him and pulls me forward for a kiss. "You're on top now. Just move however it feels good for you."

My cheeks are still burning red. Camouflage be damned. His hand holds my hip firmly while his other runs gently along my inner thigh. His long fingers move along my body smoothly, moving in and out of my lady parts before he shifts me slightly closer to his penis. He stretches up for a kiss, giving me some tongue as his hands press me down. His erection enters me at my pace and I exhale with molten bliss. He fills me and my eyes close in wanton pleasure. His hands move to mine again, helping me keep my balance as I move slowly on top of him.

"Is this okay?" I ask in a rough voice.

"Babe, this has never felt better."

Encouraged I move a little faster, build up a pace that's gratifying for both of us. Up and down, slightly forward then repeat. I love the repeat part. My hands fall to his muscular chest and I keep myself upright and moving. I forget about everything, all my doubts and fears. The pleasure he's giving me is overwhelming and intense. I'm rocking back and forth when I'm seized by my orgasm and call out to his deity relative's and his name, "Oh, God, Will!" He follows me into the abyss a moment later when he comes.

"Lauren," he says in a quiet voice. I dreamily look up from his chest as he asks, "Tell me something, at your age why don't you have more experience with men?"

I lay my head back on his chest, "It's by choice." I leave it at that.

The room is dark and bitterly cold. I'm shivering and realize I'm naked. Have I been sleeping? I don't remember falling asleep. I look up and observe an empty room. The old window on the far wall has been broken. Chunks of glass that lay scattered on the wooden floor glint with shallow light from the moon. It's eerily silent except for the whistling winter wind I can hear outside. I'm not in a house, a barn maybe? I'm having trouble sitting up. I lift my hands in front of me and gasp at the sight of chains. I've been chained, bound by leather shackles to my wrists. Fear seizes me. I fumble to get the bindings off. I can't get them off, I can't, I don't know how. The barn door opens.

Pressure lands on my shoulder and I throw myself across the bed.

"Lauren!"

I'm caught between sleep and consciousness as I scramble away. I fall off the bed and land hard on the wood floor. "Ah, fuck!" I shout and roll onto my back. Fucking nightmare. Tears stream across my face.

Will's face appears over me as he comes to the edge of the bed, "Shit! What was that?"

I struggle to sit up and he stretches to turn on my nightstand lamp.

"It was a fucking nightmare. Shit, sorry." I'm sitting up on the floor by the bed but still struggling to control the frenzied emotions that are left. He offers his hand and I move back onto the bed. I press a shaking palm to my forehead. I hit it hard.

"Your arm's bleeding again," he gets out of the bed and goes into the darkened bathroom. He returns quickly with a damp washcloth. "Let me look," he says taking my arm. "You're shaking," he observes, mildly pissed. He turns my arm over and gently wipes the blood away. "I think you pulled a stitch or two."

"I don't want to go back to the hospital. Can we just stick a Band-Aid on it?"

"Yeah, come on."

He walks me into the bathroom and turns the light on. It momentarily blinds me as he leads me across to the sink. He wipes my arm again and presses the washcloth to my torn skin as he searches the cabinet for the Band-Aid box. He takes one and sets the box down on the counter. He strips the bandage of its packaging and removes the washcloth. Tugging slightly on the broken stitches he removes them. I hardly notice. He pulls the bandage over the area the stitches have vacated. Taking a quick look at my forehead he announces that I'll probably have a black and blue in the morning.

"I think you missed your calling Mr. Rysberg," I say quietly.

He presses a kiss to my arm then my forehead and looks up at me with sad, knowing eyes. "Let's see if we can get some sleep. I have to work in the morning."

I nod and follow him back to bed. He holds up the comforter and I crawl in but just to his side. I want to be close. He lies behind me and pulls me tight to him, my back to his chest. He tucks the comforter around our bodies and swiftly turns off my lamp. He shifts my pillow and holds me close. I exhale and realize in the dark, surrounded by this gorgeous, kind man, I'm still shaking.

Chapter 7

The alarm is buzzing and I hate it.

It silences quickly and I fall back to sleep in the predawn world. I roll over as the bed sinks and shifts under his returning weight. Willem kisses my forehead and says, "I'm gone to work babe. A man's got to make a living."

"Work?" I mumble, not understanding the concept.

"Yep," he's smiling in the dark, I can tell without opening my eyes, "I've got a photo-shoot this morning. I'm going to be on the cover of *Men's Monthly* next month."

I touch his arm, "Okay, I'll buy the issue." I smile in the dark and am rewarded with a deep kiss.

"See you at the audition. Remember you have to go in the morning. Don't sleep in. I'm leaving you the Maserati to drive. Keys are in the kitchen. Be careful."

"'K," I roll over and hug his pillow.

Driving…and me, not a good combination. Just because I have a license doesn't mean I know how to use it. I type in Nicole's address in the navigation system and wait. I've fixed the seat, the mirrors, but am fearful about everything involving the pricey car. The metallic voice announces the direction so I put the car in reverse and start to go. I brake hard finding a closed garage door in the rearview mirror. Shaking my head, I remind myself that I'm stupid and push the garage door opener. As I wait for it to open I look to the empty car space beside the Maserati. There was an old red Ford truck parked there, it's gone to the photo-shoot. I want to go to the photo-shoot. Some lucky person gets to take pictures of Willem in the early morning sun. I'm sure he's looking fantastic for the camera and can't wait to ask him a thousand questions about his morning. When the door is completely open I back out into the driveway and close it.

Arriving at Nicole's house almost seems like déjà vu, the driveway gate is open and a few high end cars are parked around the circle, except this time I'm driving and a round driveway freaks me out. I can imagine myself hitting every car in the driveway trying to make the roundabout turn. Fortunately there's a space along the sidewalk and I slow the vehicle to a crawl and pull in. The tire hits the curbing so I know I'm close. I back up, straighten it out and try again to the sound of just a little bit of metal scrapping. When I know I've parked close enough I get out and inspect the damage. There's a few scrapes to the tire and the rim but nothing serious, Will may not even notice.

I walk through the driveway gate and ring the doorbell. Nicole answers the door sans the margarita in her hand. She takes me in a big hug and immediately asks how I'm feeling, is my arm is any better? I pronounce myself healthy but she looks at the black and blue on my forehead and grimaces. I regard her and announce, "You got the memo."

She looks me over and matches my grin. We've almost coordinated our clothing today. We're both wearing khaki pants and button-up purple shirts. Hers is a burgundy which brings out the richness of her dark skin, while mine's pansy purple in a gingham print.

"Great minds think alike," she says taking me gently by the arm.

Leading me into the house again we stop in the kitchen. My eyes go wide, "Wow! Those are beautiful!" A large bouquet of flowers with hues of purples, blues and whites is sitting on the granite counter in a crystal vase. "You're so lucky, I never get flowers." Envy pops up its ugly head and growls.

"Those aren't mine, they're yours." She's amused. Smiling she says, "Ethan sent them when he heard you'd gotten hurt. He didn't know which hotel you're staying at. I don't give out that kind of information, so he sent them here." She leans into the bouquet for a sniff, "Mmm, they are wonderful!" She leans back and says, "You're the last one to show up." I murmur something about traffic. I decide not to tell her that I drive like a frightened eight year old. "No worries," she says in her best fake Australian accent.

"The Aussie's entertaining us," she's laughing and walking, "and Maria."

"Do you like her for the film?" I ask as we pass by where I spilled my blood the other day. There is no remaining evidence of my clumsiness.

"We'll see after the auditions," she says over her shoulder.

We return to the work room. I give my hellos to everyone and apologize about the damn LA traffic making me late. I'm such a liar. I retrieve my iPad from my purse and turn it on for the first time since our horrific accident. I keep so much stuff on it I'm fearful it won't recover as quickly as I have from our fall. I press the on button and pray. I give a cheer when it fires up. I look up to see many eyes on me, I smile and point, "It's working." No one appreciates this but me. I get quiet as the actors go to work.

I'm writing my notes rather than talking or contributing but everything I'm writing about Cole seems to end up with him as the lead for my next book. For Maria, I see a hint of her Latino heritage in her almond eyes and almost black hair. She's exquisite and talented but I'm fifty-fifty about her for the female role. I'm curious to see what the others will have to say.

The audition lasts about an hour when Todd gives them the same line about talking behind their backs. Everyone is saying their goodbyes when I speak up, "I know this really isn't planned but can I talk with Cole in private?"

They look at me and make comments about needing to give us some time. Nicole eyes me suspiciously and points to her ring finger as if reminding me he's married. I stick my tongue out at her, very eight year old like before she shuts the door.

"What's up, love?" Cole asks me.

I point to one of the small couches and start messing around with my iPad. I keep all of my books in there, including the new one. I'm searching and look up into his chocolate brown eyes as we sit, "I hope you're okay with me asking you to stay." He tells me it's fine as I find what I'm looking for. I focus on him, "I'd like you to read something for me. Don't worry about getting the words exactly right, I just have an idea and I want to hear you."

"OK love, let me see."

I pass over the top-secret information and take a deep breath. "This is the copy of my next book that's at the editor's right now. So, when it comes back completely finished this might be different. What I want you to read might not even be in there anymore."

He looks over the paragraph and looks to me, "Can you tell me about the character, the scene?"

"He's a being that's been stuck between Heaven and Hell, meeting his eternal love again, the first time in a thousand years, at a night club."

His smile lights up his eyes, "Excellent." He hands me back the iPad. A deep breath and he starts, his accent has disappeared, "When I was a young man, a very long time ago," he smiles and my heart momentarily stops. "God was vengeful, a punisher. He did not forgive as your generation believes He does now. For punishment of my sins, he took me from my life on Earth. He placed me where I could watch you. It was my only saving grace," he says, "Watching you; it saw me through the most difficult times. I kept my sanity because of you. I was able to remember what it was to be human but," he takes a ragged breath, "I watched you die more than a hundred times."

He quiets and I break into a huge smile. I've found my man, literally speaking. "That was awesome," I declare. "I don't want you for this movie," he looks as if I've wounded him so I quickly add, "I want you for the next. For my next book, the one coming out in the spring. You are exactly who I want for that role. I hope this doesn't disappoint you."

"Work is work, I'll be happy to have this movie or the next." He stands from the couch, "You'll keep me in mind when the time comes." I agree and tell him he won't have any competition at that time, "I'll expect a copy of the book in the spring then," he says with a huge, friendly smile.

We walk to the kitchen where Cole says goodbye to the others.

"What was that about?" Nicole asks. Todd peers over her shoulder as if to ask the same question.

"I don't want Cole for this movie." We settle around the kitchen table and I tell them, "I want him for the next book, if you end up making it a movie. I had him go through a paragraph of my book just to see him say the words. He's perfect for it. I can't have him in this movie and then the next, so I want him for the next."

"Are you sure?" Nicole asks. I stress again that he needs to be considered for the next book to movie. A murmur goes around the table; I've thrown them a curve ball. We talk of their audition and they move onto Maria since I have temporarily dismissed Cole from the prospects. "For men, that leaves Ethan and Willem." She looks at me and my eyes fall with a guilty conscience to my sandwich that someone's bought. She checks her Chanel watch, "Willem and Holly should be here soon."

I'm sitting on the little couch I had shared with Cole just a few hours before, watching the man I love work. I almost giggle with delight – but I'm an adult so I don't. We've spent countless hours together and I realize he hasn't asked me any questions about the book, the character or my motives behind the story. He doesn't want this from me; he wants the role on his own. I love him for it and I'm in awe of his talent. He's immersed into the role, making the character his own but keeping to my words, the emotions I had put to paper.

He catches my eye and I feel like I've been caught spying. A discreet wink then his smoky blue eyes return to the script. Josh is telling Holly something about how she needs to be more in tune with Will. I'm happy for her not to be. I want him for myself, character or not, even if this is his work and I feel defensive. Josh steps aside and they recreate the scene. Holly is much better having run through the lines once already.

They're almost finished when I look down at the notes I've written on my iPad. I've been doodling without realizing it. The words 'I want him' and 'I love him' are written all over the page with little flowery hearts. I glance up quickly to make sure no one has seen my love notes.

The audition finishes with a flourish and Holly pours on the extra love for her audience. She's flirty with Josh. Delicately touching Todd's arm at any given opportunity. Nicole shakes her head, not missing anything and steps to me as Willem is making himself busy with the script. I notice there's a lot of movement but nothing's being accomplished by all of his activity.

"She's kind of over the top," Nicole says quietly. I smile and agree. She turns back to the group of people, "Would anyone like a drink? In the kitchen?"

Everyone follows Nicole out of the room, funneling through the hall. Will is walking behind me, and I slow.

His hand falls gently to my hip and he leans forward whispering, "Hello beautiful." I smile over my shoulder and he pulls me to a stop. We step out of view from the hall, into some enclave of a doorway to another part of the house and his hand fists in my hair, pulling me close for a passionate kiss. His other hand runs along my curves, heating my body. He asks through kisses, "When are you coming home? I've missed you." I'm on my toes, stretching to meet every caress. I know we don't have much time, if any, before the others realize we're not with them.

"I don't know," I exhale and caress him again, "but I'll be home as soon as I can."

He smiles and presses a kiss and his body to mine then releases me quickly, "Good, I've got plans." He steps back into the hall and to the kitchen before I can gather my wits.

I know my face is flushed and my lips look puffy from the passionate assault but I can't delay my arrival. I mumble something about forgetting my iPad then walk directly to the kitchen counter for my purse. I'm pawing through my purse as an excuse not to be seen by the others. I can sense him getting closer before he speaks, but not to me. Nicole is walking next to Willem as I turn from the counter to find them beside me.

She points to the bouquet and says, "Ethan sent Lauren flowers when he found out she had gotten hurt. Aren't they beautiful?"

He leans to them and inhales, "They're lovely." He stares at me and says, "I should have been more thoughtful, I didn't get you anything." I shrink under his direct stare and flush thinking of every time he's given me his body. "Nicole dear," he leans to her and kisses her cheek, "I have to go. Please give me a call when a decision's been made." From her he leans to me, "Lauren, my love," my heart faints onto the tile floor, "It's been a wonderful experience meeting you." He presses his soft lips to my cheek, lingering. He steps away quickly; saying goodbye to the others before he leaves.

Nicole's fanning herself with her hand exaggeratedly, "I think it just got hot in here!" She's all-out chuckling, "Your face is so red!" I playfully swat at her as I watch him close the door.

The house feels empty without him. I feel empty without him.

We're huddling around the kitchen table. The casting agents are fawning over pictures that are strewn about. Josh reaches for a picture of Will, (I sigh over the splendor the picture contains) and says, "With Cole out I think Willem is the best actor."

Nicole pipes in, "Ethan's great too but his agent is demanding a lot of money for him."

"How much?" I ask.

"He wants fifteen million." I almost fall out of my chair.

"Ladies first. What about Kate?" Todd asks seriously. "Her last filmed bombed."

"OK, she's out," Nicole says with the finality of a hatchet man. She looks to me, "What do you think Lauren?"

"I like Holly but I think Maria was really good too." They talk over options. Did they want to bring her back, have her work through the script with Willem? I point out, "I don't have much more time in LA. I won't be able to watch any more auditions."

"No more auditions," Todd advises. "We'll just piece together who we want from what they've done. Josh, what do you think? Pick a lady."

"I like Maria too. She's got the depth for the script. She's going to need it for the character."

"Nicole," Todd asks, "what's your opinion?"

"Cost wise, she's good, right at three million."

"How did her last film do?" he asks her.

Nicole passes over a sheet full of statistics, "It's hard to say because she didn't carry the film on her name only. Her male lead was Ryan Bauer." There's a general buzz around the table, everyone knows Ryan Bauer.

Todd accepts the paperwork and reviews it quickly. He sets it aside, "OK, I'm fine with this. So everyone's opinion is Maria for the female lead?"

Todd asks to nodding heads around the table. He looks to one of the casting agents, "Alright, go call her agent. Offer her the three and have him check her schedule for summer filming. Call the other ladies agents, advise them of our decline." The agent's on his cell phone before Todd can breathe again. "Now for the men," he looks right at me, "You sure about Cole?" I confirm that I am. Todd smiles, "I want first option on that next book of yours."

"That's between you and my agent," I grin.

He laughs, moving back to the real focus, "Tell me what you think about the men."

Nicole looks up from her notes, eyeing me curiously.

"I, ah," I fumble as Nicole hides her smile, "I think fifteen million for a salary is a lot."

"Don't you want to know how much Willem's agent is asking before you decide how much is too much?" she asks me with faux innocence. The depth of her inquisitiveness is endless. OK, sure, I should probably know that. Nicole continues but looks back to Todd, "His agent's asking ten million."

"That's not bad," Todd says leaning back.

Josh comments, "If we're talking just acting skills, not salaries, Willem is the better actor than Ethan. He's done the hard work before and done it well. Ethan is the action star, the fighter. I'm not sure he can handle the more emotional scenes."

"Can Willem handle the action scenes?" Todd asks.

"Physically," Josh says, "I don't think that's a problem. He's in good shape. We can hire trainers. Teach him how to fight if we need to."

I raise my hand, jeez; I feel like I'm back in school and set my hand down. The others turn to me, "Sweden has mandatory military service, or at least it did when he was younger. He would've had to serve."

"How do you know that?" Josh asks.

"I lived there, everyone knew about the conscription." I add, "It's not in effect anymore."

"So he should know at least the basics," Todd adds.

"And even if we hire a team of trainers to get him fighting again we'll still spend less than we will on Ethan alone," Nicole comments. "Do you want to add anything, Lauren?"

Now or never, this is what Anne argued for, my creative influence. I just have to say his name. Say it and have the movie tied to gossip forever.

Nicole leans close and whispers in my ear, "It's okay, you can want him for the movie and like him personally. You're both adults. They want him for the movie. Can't you tell the decision's been made? They just want your approval." Miss Know It All.

"Okay," I lean back from her, "I agree with Josh, Willem is the better actor. I think acting skills will be more important, but I'll leave it to your judgment."

Todd makes the final decision, and looks to the other casting agent, "Make the call to his agent, agree to his salary but I want him available for whenever the filming schedule's set. Call Ethan's, and Cole's agents, just so it's official. Let them know we've gone with Willem." He stands and stretches his hand to me. I accept it as he says, "Good doing business with you Lauren."

"You too, Todd," I receive a little squeeze to my hand.

"Nicole will keep in touch with you and Anne. We'll get you over the dates for the shooting schedule, eventually the film's release date."

"Thank you," my creative influence comes to an end.

Chapter 8

The hotel is my next destination after I leave Nicole's house. I park the car in the underground garage and take the elevator to the lobby. A short walk across the foyer to the main set of elevators and I'm humming to the background music the whole way up. Back in the room I've hardly used I begin the process for checking out.

I sit on the edge of the bed and call Anne. It goes straight to voicemail so I leave her a message telling her that they've picked Willem and Maria for the movie roles, and that yes, I'm happy with the decision. I tell her not to believe anything she sees on TMZ, (without explaining the comment) and that I really am alright from the fall.

I hang up and toss the cell into my purse. It takes thirty minutes to pack my big black bag with everything from my good dresses and shoes to the toiletry things Willem didn't bring back to the house. I check the room once more to make sure I have everything of mine before I zip up my bag, grab my purse and catch the elevator to the main floor.

At the lobby desk I sign for the credit card charge and get a copy of the invoice in return. I stare at the cost but can't consider it wasted money. Here or at Willem's house, I've really enjoyed my trip to California.

"Hey there clumsy," a voice says behind me.

I glance over my shoulder and smile finding Ethan behind me. I turn quickly back and thank the lady for the receipt and grab the handle of my roller bag. I pull it to the side, out of the way and say, "Hi Ethan, it's good to see you again. Thank you for the flowers, they're beautiful."

"But you don't have them with you?" he observes.

"No, I can't take them with me on the flight, so I left them at Nicole's. I think I would have had to fight her for them anyway. Are you seeing someone at the hotel?"

He shrugs, "I came to see you."

A red warning light goes off in my mind.

"Do you want to get a drink?" He points over his shoulder to the hotel bar.

"I'm driving, I better not."

"Yeah, I saw you driving his Maserati." He smiles that million dollar smile and says, "Just one won't hurt." He takes my suitcase from me and rolls it to the lobby desk, "Can you watch this for Ms. Radford?" I can see the giddiness of the receptionist as she talks with him, agreeing. He steps back to me, "See, no excuses now."

I turn with him and walk to the hotel bar. He orders a beer and I ask for a bottle of water. The bartender passes the order over and is close by wiping down the counter just past me. I shift in my seat and face Ethan.

He sips the beer then says in a quiet voice, "So, your fucking Will just cost me fifteen million dollars." All the blood drains from my face, I'm abruptly cold.

He's pissed; my red warning light has become a strobe light.

"I didn't make the decision, Ethan. I was just part of the process," I manage to say.

All of his playfulness has been lost. He leans to me and hisses, "Fifteen…million…dollars. You gave him the role because he's been busy between your legs. He must be a great fuck or you just have really low standards. Didn't anyone warn you about Hollywood?" His hand settles on my thigh and my Icky Scale shoots over the top. "If I'd gotten to you first, would you have given me the part?"

My insides turn icy with panic. My façade is almost breaking as I lift his hand from my leg. I look at the bartender, "Can you call hotel security?" I turn back to Ethan, "Leave me the fuck alone or I'll have him call the police instead. Which do you prefer the paparazzi get a picture of, you leaving the hotel? Or you leaving the hotel in cuffs? Your decision."

A pay-by-hour security guard steps to me, "Can I help you with something, Miss?"

I stare into the hatred of Ethan's eyes, "Willem's my friend, you assume too much about our relationship. Get over yourself." I turn to the guard,

"Mr. Dash needs some help leaving the hotel. Can you show him out?"

"Sure," he takes Ethan's arm, giving him a slight jerk to get him out of his chair and moving, "Come on, Sir."

"Get your fucking hands off me!" Ethan orders the guard. "Bitch," he spits at me before stalking off.

My façade breaks and I take a sip of the water with a shaky hand. I wait until I've calmed a little, enough time to make sure Ethan's gone before I put a bill on the bar and walk back to the lobby desk. The receptionist smiles and I tell her, "I need to get my bag." She steps quickly away and rolls my bag from the back. "Can I have a guard walk me to my car?" I'm not the least bit embarrassed to ask.

"Of course, Ms. Radford." She lifts the desk phone and orders the guard to the lobby desk. Setting the phone down she says, "It will be just a moment."

I make it to the Maserati and the guard helps me put the bag into the trunk. I thank him and look around the garage as I get into the car. My warning censors are buzzing like a nuclear warning device in Chernobyl. As I drive out of the parking garage I'm looking around every corner, behind every car.

A shadow runs towards the car and I brake hard. A rock shatters the passenger window spraying glass everywhere. I gun the car out of the garage and into traffic, not even slowing down to look. I push the bits of glass off of me and curse. It's a few blocks before I slow down my speeding and my heart rate. I press the home button on the navigation system and follow it as it leads me back to Willem.

I open the kitchen garage door and step in with my purse. I'm pissed and upset as I walk over to the sink.

Will looks up from the stove; he's waving an oven mitt over a steaming pot. He smiles and says in Swedish, "I'm making Inkokt Lax. This is really exciting since I don't cook much." He sees my face and switches to English, "If I'd known you were going to be pissed about me cooking I would have made us reservations."

I glance over my shoulder, "I'm not pissed at you and I like boiled salmon." I shake my purse over the sink dropping everything into it. My things clank around the stainless steel. I give another good shake trying to get out the pieces of glass.

He comes and stands behind me wrapping an arm around my waist and he looks over my shoulder into the sink. "What are you doing? Is that glass?"

"Yes, that's glass."

"Did you have an accident?" he's concerned. Worried about me or his beautiful Maserati? He tosses the oven mitt to the counter and moves closer, "What happened?" I drop my purse into the sink and turn for him, wrapping my arms around him. I bury my face into his chest and sigh with relief as his arms tighten. Safe, I feel safe in his arms.

"I'm so sorry," I say to his chest. "I owe you a window. Supper smells wonderful incidentally." He looks down at me with those eyes that always make me melt. Since there's lots of car damage I fess up, "I might owe you a tire too but that's only because I'm a lousy parker."

"What happened?" he asks and takes my hand. He leads me back into the garage and stands there looking forlorn at the broken vehicle.

"I had a run in with Ethan Dash at the hotel." He looks expectant so I keep talking, "I went to the hotel to checkout since I'm staying here. He caught me at the lobby desk and wanted to talk." My shoulders slump recalling my anxiety. "He said some awful things about me and you and you getting the role."

"I heard he can be a prick about things. I'm sorry."

I look up at him, "Congratulations by the way,"

"Thank you." There's no enthusiasm in his voice. "Where's your bag?" I tell him it's in the trunk. He pops the button on the center console by reaching through the broken window. "Don't worry about it Lauren. It's all fixable. He's a shit, don't worry about him." He pulls the black bag from the trunk and sets it just inside the kitchen door. He returns to stand by me. "Do you want me to call the police? Or just go beat the shit out of him?" There's no hint of a smile. He's serious.

I shake my head, "No, you can't beat him up."

"Are you sure? Because I'd really love to kick his ass right now."

The possibility oddly lifts my spirits, making me smile, "No, you can't." I sigh with regret, "I didn't see him throw the rock so you can't call the cops. It happened so fast I just didn't see him, but I know he did it. He was so pissed about losing his paycheck." I look pitifully at the car and offer, "I'll pay for the window and the tire. I can buy you a new one if you want."

"A new what?" he asks.

"A new Maserati, if you want."

He chuckles and leans in for a kiss. "No one's ever offered me that." He laughing as he says, "Go inside, check on my fish." I walk across the garage to the door and glance over my shoulder. He's hugging his car, telling her she'll be okay. Boys and their fast, broken toys.

Mashed carrots, boiled potatoes and boiled salmon, I haven't had a good home cooked meal in forever and I tell him he's the best cook ever. That earns me a kiss.

"Is that what you were planning earlier?" I ask.

"Yes, I've been skimping on meals for you. I wanted to go all out and make something from home."

I've eaten everything he's put on my plate. I am satisfied but looking at him I find a new hunger growing. "I'm really happy you got the part."

"Was it you? Were you the deciding vote?"

"Actually I gave them my opinion but left it up to them. I told them you were the best actor there. They agreed with me." He nods accepting the brief version. I stand and take our plates to the kitchen counter. "You cooked so I'll clean." He takes the empty wine glasses and moves them to the counter next to my glass-free purse. The contents have been tossed back in minus the glass bits.

"I can help too."

I start the hot water running as he moves pots and pans to the sink for cleaning. I begin with the plates. Hot, bubbly water feels good on my skin as I wash them, rinse and then set the dishes aside to dry. He presses a kiss to my neck as he stands behind me. One kiss becomes many and I tilt my head to the side, giving him better access to my freckled skin. The soft pressure of his lips to my neck sends ripples of passion through my body.

I mutter something about it feeling good and his hands wrap around my waist. He steps closer and pulls me tighter as a hand moves up to my breast giving it a playful squeeze. "The dishes will not get done if you keep that up," I warn. He's unbuttoning my purple shirt as I stretch over my shoulder for a kiss a la *Titanic* minus the dolphins and icebergs. He dunks his hands in the soapy water and I gasp with pleasure as his wet hands find my bare stomach and breasts. "You're teasing me," I say in agony, turning around in his arms. I wrap my arms around his neck as he lifts me onto the kitchen counter.

"If anything, beautiful, I am not a tease."

Then he proves it, on the kitchen counter and again on the kitchen floor.

I'm lying naked on the kitchen floor giggling like a school girl and I adore it. He makes me feel so...loved...so happy and safe.

"What time is it?" I ask.

"Why?" His leg is draped over mine, his hand rests on my stomach.

"I have a thing to go to. I want you to go with me."

"Not another date with a comedian?"

I roll onto him and press kisses to his muscular chest and neck, "No, it's a charity thing. Downtown. We don't have to stay long but Anne put it on my schedule of to-dos in California."

"A dress up thing?" I nod and he asks, "You have a dress?" I nod again. He sits up taking me with him and says, "OK, let's go have fun."

I shower quickly, not getting my hair wet. I playfully avoid the offers of help Willem gives me. If I accept we'll never go out. He steps into the shower as soon as I step out and says, "I've called for a ride since the Maserati's out of commission for a while. It'll be here in about thirty minutes, is that okay?"

"Yep, that's enough time." I'm not fixing my hair so it's plenty of time. I run a brush through it. I do it again, then again, not quite happy with the results. Deciding on something different I braid it. Coiling the braid at the base of my neck I pin it together. I like the look. I sneak peeks of Willem in the shower, the outline of his naked body calls to my hoochie beckoning it closer and I barely resist temptation. I put on a little make-up and realize I have taken over his bathroom counter without any complaints. It makes me beam with untold happiness.

I hang up the white towel on the rack before I leave the bathroom. I'm walking around naked, completely at ease in his home, in his bedroom. My bag is unzipped and laying on my side of the bed. He's so sweet to do that for me. I take out my black dress. It's a little thing with a big price tag. I got it special for the trip. I put on my strapless black bra and hold up my black thong panties. These are going to drive him crazy later. I wiggle into them and sit on the edge of the bed.

I put on my thigh-high silk stockings, one leg at a time then take my fancy shoes from the bag. They're sky high black patent leather pumps with cork heels. They are the coolest high heels I've ever seen. I give them a hug, holding them to my chest in complete adoration. "I love you, my precious," I say sounding a little too much like Gollum.

My attention is drawn away from the shoes to the bathroom door. Willem is standing at the threshold with a towel around his waist. He looks good enough to eat. He's smirking at me, "I thought you were supposed to be in love with me, not shoes."

"I am in love with you," I say before thinking. My stomach hits the floor. My heart runs screaming from the room. I add, trying to make it all a joke, "And my shoes. Hope you don't mind." I'm an idiot. Stupid, I chide myself, so stupid.

He slowly walks to me and kneels down, taking the shoes from my hands. He lifts my left foot and places the heel on it. He repeats with my right foot. He sets my feet on the floor and spreads my legs. He's quiet as he leans forward for a kiss and says, "Only me. Not your shoes, not anyone else, okay?"

He's pressing kisses to my neck. The stroke of his tongue sends shivers across my freckled skin. A kiss is placed to the curve of my breast as it sits pushed up in the strapless bra. I hold his head to my chest, running my fingers through his soft, wet blonde hair. My heart is pounding. He keeps his kisses moving south and his lips press against my panties. A skillful finger of his pushes the lacy edge aside and my adrenaline spikes. His tongue finds my softest spot and I moan. His tongue is merciless as he kisses and licks and sucks. I fall backwards on the bed with a throaty exhale of pleasure.

This is definitely love.

His long fingers enter my wetness and grind against me. My knees pull up in response to his movement. My heels rest on his shoulders as he keeps going. His tongue is swirling my clit and my body rushes with pleasure. I come so hard I worry I've hurt him. I prop myself up on my elbows and look along my body to him. He stands and leans over me to the comforter. He wipes my come off of his mouth and beams. Returning to me he presses a deep kiss to my lips and smiles as he pulls the towel away from his waist, "I'm in love with you too."

"Even the crazy parts of me?" I worry out loud.

"Yes, even those." He throws the towel to the floor and shows me how much he loves me.

Chapter 9

It doesn't matter that we're late for the charity event. Late is the norm in LA. It's just Willem and I alone in a sea of people. He's concentrating only on me, hanging on my every word. Just the way I like it. Occasionally the bubble expands around us as we talk with others, mingling with the well-dressed crowd. For the most part, it's just us and it's more than enough.

The party is being thrown at an old railway station that's been refurbished for a youth arts center. Anne thought my presence would be a good thing for the charity. At the time she accepted the invitation she never considered getting a plus one. Having Willem by my side is a good thing, not just for me but for the charity as well.

The renovated space is enormous. The ceiling is made up of numerous frosted glass panels that someone has propped open with some kind of antiquated mechanism allowing the heat below to dissipate into the evening stars. The main level is old-fashioned art deco with tiled floors. Linen tables of champagne and appetizers are at one end while children's' artwork line the walls which adds color to the vanilla-colored expanse.

Willem takes two glasses of champagne from a tray as a waiter walks by and hands me one. I take a long pull as we walk towards the far end of the building. This area is closer to the working offices of the charity and the restrooms. There are darkened halls that spread out in different directions but those are closed off for the event. Obviously someone didn't want guests wandering out of the main lobby area and getting lost during the event. Preventative measures.

Will leans to me and says, "You are beautiful in that dress." It's a basic black dress that's more like a long, tight tube shirt than a dress. Somewhat on the slutty side starting just at my breasts and ending at mid-thigh but Will seems happy with it and that makes me intensely happy. I return the compliment; he looks fantastic in a black suit and tie. His crisp white shirt pops beneath the dark tie. We're standing away from the crowd, partially hidden in the darkened hall as he whispers, "Come on." He nods over his shoulder to an area that's been quartered off with a velvety rope. He steps over the rope.

"Show off," I shout after him as he walks further into the darkened building. I glance around and find no one noticing us with our naughty behavior so I duck under the rope and follow him into the obscurity.

He's walking casually ahead of me as I jog a little to catch up which is quite the feat in the heels I'm wearing. "You're so bad," I chastise with a smile. He checks a door along the hall and finds it unlocked. We step inside and he closes the door behind me.

"I just wanted some alone time with you." He sets his glass down and steps close. His hands find my hips and I stand tall for a kiss. His hands direct me backward, shuffling me across the room to where my legs find a couch. He finally kisses me and switches places. He sits down on the couch and I'm left standing over him. "What are you going to do with me Ms. Radford, now that you have me here?" As if this was all my idea. My mind runs the gamut, what could I do with him? To him? To him gives me an idea.

I lean forward, giving him a great view of the girls. I pull his silky tie to me for a kiss on those fantastic lips of his then releasing it he reclines into the couch with a grin. I'm not exactly sure what I'm doing but the general idea is pretty basic. He's the lollipop and I'm going to suck on the candy.

I'm on my knees in front of him and undo his black belt then the zipper. His erection is released and I run my hand up and down his shaft. He closes his eyes and his head flops back onto the couch. He's mine to use and lovingly abuse. I lean forward and press a kiss to his hardness. A moan escapes his lips and it's encouraging. My mouth waters and my lips part. I slide him further into my mouth. At the bottom of his shaft my hand tightens its grip and my mouth slides along. I move upward and twirl my tongue as I go.

He's whispering in Swedish again, all about the pleasure he's experiencing and a smile reaches my busy mouth. His hands entwine in my hair as my lips go down again. "Watch the hair," I say sternly then return to my pleasure. I repeat the motion several times, very slowly then with a little more confidence I suck harder, pick up my pace. I know he's enjoying it as his grip on my hair tightens. He says something about coming soon but I'm enjoying myself too much to care. His hips push forward on me and I swallow everything he gives.

I lean back and ask, "Was that okay?"

"Okay?" he repeats. "That was unbelievable."

I smile and stand, "They say the first time's always memorable."

He zips his pants up and says, "What do you mean?"

I walk over to my glass of champagne and swallow down the rest of it. My mouth perks at the sweetness. "I haven't done that before." He looks at me as if I've grown elephant ears, "Can we do that again? I really like that."

He takes me into a hard hug and presses a kiss to my neck that makes me giggle, "Absolutely."

We work our way back into the crowded lobby. No one seems to have noticed our disappearance and reappearance. He holds my hand as we walk through the mass of people. He's warm and strong. He makes me feel safe and loved. Leaning to me and he says, "I'm starving. Let's get something from the table."

I pick up a little blue ceramic plate and walk along the table picking and choosing a few little things. I'm not that hungry since he made me a wonderful dinner. Off to the side five members of an orchestra are playing. The soft tunes of Pachelbel's "Cannon" whisper through the area. Willem's leaning in, talking of things that only lovers talk of. I cautiously glance around to make sure he's not being heard. He promises something later and I smile up at him, accepting his offer when I realize something's not quite right.

I look at my plate and turn from Willem, leaving him where he stands. I set my plate on the table and point to an appetizer asking the attendant, "What's in this?"

"It's prosciutto on a wheat toast with boiled egg and hollandaise, Miss."

I swallow hard.

"What is it?" Willem asks as he steps to my side.

I'm overwhelmed by dread. The last time I had an anaphylactic episode it was really bad. I was left lying on the floor barely breathing…completely alone, the memory is chilling. I look up at him, "The appetizer had egg in it. I ate it." I look over the crowd, remembering where the bathroom is, "Excuse me." I step away from him and walk quickly through the mass of bodies. I rush into the ladies room and he follows me in. "You're not supposed to be in here," I warn.

"Bullshit," he says. Direct and to the point. I like that.

I open my clutch and hand him my EpiPen. "Have you ever used one of these?" He accepts the injector and says that he hasn't. "OK, you remember John Travolta in *Pulp Fiction* where he stabs the girl in the heart?"

"Yeah, OK," he shifts the injector in his hand holding it like he's going to stab me with it. Yikes, *Psycho* shower scene moment.

I grab his hand, "Don't do it like that!" I look around the bathroom and find the trashcan. "This is going to be messy." I hand him my clutch and give him one more chance, "Are you sure you want to stay? I have to throw up. It's going to be gross. You can leave, it'll be alright." Silently, I'm begging him not to go.

As soon as he says that he's not leaving again I walk to the trashcan and bend over. What hair has fallen (or been pulled – thank you very much) from my braid I push out of my face and he holds it back further for my benefit. I take a few deep breaths working up my courage then shove my finger to the back of my throat.

My eyes squeeze tight as I vomit. The acid burns my throat as I puke up my guts. Snacks, dinner, even the most intimate parts of Willem come up. I throw up a few more times before my stomach finally rests. I feel like I've been hit with a truck. I wipe the tears from my eyes and step to the sink. I rinse my mouth in the fresh water and spit a few times. I turn to find his eyes on me. "I'm sorry, I know that was terrible. I just needed to get what I could of the egg out of my body."

"You're not the first person I've seen throw up."

I wipe my mouth on a paper towel and say, "I usually have fifteen minutes before I go down. Give or take five minutes and we'll know if I have an attack."

"I should take you to the hospital," he says.

"Really? You think you're going to get me to a hospital twice in one week? Not going to happen." Stubborn and crazy is not a good combination.

We leave the bathroom behind and walk back towards the dark hall where all of our fun had occurred earlier in the night. In a very unladylike move I sit on the floor and lean back against the cool wall. Willem sits beside me, my clutch and the EpiPen in his hands.

I lean my head against his shoulder and we sit there quietly while time ticks by. Finally I say, "I don't feel good." I point to the injector and wheeze, "Unscrew the little cap. That end goes in my thigh." I wheeze again, "Its pressure sensitive so as soon as you press it to my leg the plunger will lower, that's all you have to do." I gasp for a breath. "OK Will."

He sits up and hikes the skirt of my dress over the lacy edge of my stocking and presses it to my skin. The plunger sinks in forcing the medicine into my system. I wheeze again and lean my head back against the tile wall. His hand tilts my face upward, "Tell me how you're feeling."

I give a slow breath, "I'm better." I take in a long, slow lungful of air. I grasp his hand in mine. Its two more breaths before I actually feel like I'm telling the truth. The medicine's swirling around my body, releasing the tightened muscles around my esophagus. Time passes us by quietly as we sit together on the tile floor until I actually do feel better. "I want to leave now. I'm OK."

He stands and reaches for me, setting me gently on my pretty patent leather heels and takes my arm. I don't think there's anyone we need to say goodbye to so we walk directly out into the crisp fall air. I instantly feel better with the cool air biting at my face and throat. His hand never leaves mine as he talks with the valet. Our ride comes forward and he opens the door for me. I climb into the black Yukon, a very unCalifornialike gas hog.

I lean my head against Willem's shoulder the whole way home. He removes his tie and stuffs it in his pocket then loosens a few buttons. He presses a kiss to my forehead and holds my hand within his over his heart. He asks again, "Are you sure you don't want to go to the hospital?"

"I just want to go home." Home with him.

"Do you want anything?" he asks, "Tea? Something soothing?" His jacket is thrown over the couch and he's standing in the kitchen looking for something to do. He's hovering like a mother hen, overwhelming me. The hiss of a voice returns in my mind and it screams 'PISS OFF!' It's been days of quiet, of peace. I press my fingers to my temple, trying to force them away. I've been good; we've been good for days. I don't understand why the voices can't stay away.

"I'm not fragile, Will." Sure, I've proven I can fall like it's an Olympic sport...several times but...I finally understand I am what he implies. I need to take the words back. I am mentally and physically fragile...weak. That's how he sees me, someone in constant need of being taken care of. Someone who needs to be comforted and it hurts my feelings, as if the contemptuous voices aren't enough.

He closes the door to the bathroom, separating us. I change out of my dress and pretty underthings quickly. I don't want him to see me naked. I don't want any pity. The voices are screaming again. I stop momentarily to press my palm to my forehead. My eyes are watering from the splitting headache they're giving me.

I throw on the t-shirt I've claimed as my own and my pale blue flannel sleeping shorts with puffy white clouds. I've had them so long they've turned super soft and smell of the fabric softener I use at home. I unknot my hair quickly, tossing the pins onto my dress and rush for the kitchen. I grab my iPad from my big purse off the island and hurry back to the bedroom. It's now or never. I am not fragile. I am not. I'm not...really.

He's out of the bathroom and leaning back against the headboard of the bed when I return. He looks much better in his t-shirt and flannel pj's than I do. I shake my head, forcing the voices quiet and sit on the bed, far enough away that he can't reach out and touch me.

I take a deep breath and fire up my iPad. I have the articles in a folder and open it up. It's the first time the folder's been opened in years, maybe ever, since I loaded it when I bought the iPad. I look up. My erratic behavior's gotten his attention. He's waiting.

I start reading, "Eight January, eleven thirty, Stockholm." I breathe and see my hands are shaking. Stupid, fucking hands. There's nothing I can do about that now and try to focus again on the news article, "Two Teens Missing:" I try to calm my voice, my pace, "A kidnapping has been reported to Stockholm police concerning two female teens. The teens are considered to be in danger. The teens have been

126

identified as Malin Persson and Lauren Radford, both of Stockholm, both are seventeen years old. The teens were last seen in the company of a man at the Shellar grocery store parking lot on Edgarstrad. A black sedan was spotted leaving the area after a struggle with the teens. The police are asking anyone with information to call the hotline." The hotline phone number is listed in the article but I don't bother reading it.

I breathe but don't look up, my voice is unsteady and I'm trying to keep calm, "Eleven January, seven thirty, Malmo." I'm shaking harder, "Tragedy in the Missing Teens Case: In a dramatic predawn raid north of Malmo, Swedish National Police SWAT raided the farm of Stefan Reinfeldt in search for the two missing teenage girls from Stockholm, Malin Persson and Lauren Radford. Safe recovery of the Stockholm teens has been the focus of a nationwide search for days. The police received a tip from a local businessman who believed he had seen the young women in the back of a black sedan owned by local resident Johan Reinfeldt, son of Stefan Reinfeldt. A police source has confirmed that both girls were found dead, chained in a barn on the property. There were signs of horrific torture. The source advised that both Ms. Persson and Ms. Radford had been raped repeatedly," my voice fucking cracks, "and that both had suffered numerous broken bones including a fractured spine for Ms. Persson. Three men have been arrested and police are still searching for a fourth man.

It is the policy of this news organization not to release the names of rape victims, however, Ms. Persson and Ms. Radford were first identified as missing persons."

I can't meet his eyes and continue, "Eleven January, thirteen fifteen, UPDATE: Police sources have confirmed that missing Stockholm teen Lauren Radford was found alive on the Reinfeldt property. The sources advised that confusion during the early morning raid and the physical state in which Ms. Radford was found lead to the belief of her death. She has been transported to Stockholm Hospital for care."

Chapter 10

I finish reading aloud the news articles concerning my kidnapping, my death and resurrection. I bravely look up and he's sitting there, bent over his knees; palms of his hands to his face and I say, "Like Mark Twain, 'rumors of my death have been greatly exaggerated.'" I stand from the bed and leave the room.

I find myself in the kitchen and slump to the floor, leaning back against the freezer door of the refrigerator. I'm hopelessly lost. My mind quiets, there are no voices. They've disappeared in shame. Willem steps over my legs and opens the metal fridge doors above my head. I don't have the strength to look up. Cool air rushes downward, encompassing my shoulders, kissing my skin briefly before the fridge door closes. A cork pops and he steps to the counter. I hear liquid splashing into a glass but stare despairingly at the cabinet door in front of me. I feel a hollow shell.

He sits across from me on the floor, within my line of sight and hands me a glass of wine. I take it and sip. He's gotten himself a beer from the fridge too. Getting drunk seems like a good idea. I empty the wine glass in another two sips.

I jump up. My skin's crawling, alive with painful memories. The excruciating voices return with a vengeance, shredding the insides of my brain, tearing me apart. I am hideous and atrocious...a whore...slut...traitor...killer...I let her die...I killed my friend.

I throw the wine glass as hard as I can. I smash into a thousand pieces as it hits the kitchen wall. I double over screaming. I can't hear myself, only feeling the straining of my throat. My hair wrenches as I pull at its mass, trying to tear myself apart. Fuck the voices; I can do a better job of destroying myself. I'm screaming at the voices, at the men who did this, at myself. I can't stop screaming until my knees buckle.

Willem has his arms around me before I hit the floor. We're fighting, struggling. Me to get him off and him to keep me safe. He's behind me, holding me as we collapse to the kitchen floor. His arms are like a vice around me, pinning my arms to my side. The fight's gone out of me and I'm crying, saying things I have never spoken of. Eleven years of self-loathing bottled up suddenly uncork like the wine bottle he just opened.

"It's my entire fault," I finally admit. Admit to myself and to another human being. It really was all my fault. My voice is hoarse from screaming. "I wanted to go with him. I'd seen him before, at the grocery store. His name was Peter. I thought he was cute but Malin got a weird vibe from him. She knew better. I told her it would be okay. We'd just go back to his place and maybe get drunk.

"He followed us out to the parking lot, trying to talk to her, joke with her, reason with her. She told him to leave us alone and she turned her back on him. He grabbed her jacket and pulled her back. It was the palest blue jacket," my mind fragments as an IED of memories explode.

"She tried to scream but he punched her. I just stood there," I whisper. "I just stood there in the parking lot watching him hit her again and again. I'd never seen any kind of violence in real life," I whimper and cry as the memories come back painfully and anew, "Some guy got out of the car and he walked up and punched me."

Willem's head leans against my shoulder, giving me a warm spot while the rest of my body's gone cold, and I can't stop, not when I've just begun to free my soul. "When I woke up we were moving. They'd put us in the backseat of the car. I don't remember how far we traveled. I started kicking the back of the driver's seat and the guy; the passenger, he turned around and punched me again. He knocked me out completely.

"When I woke up again it was dark and I was cold and naked. We were in an abandoned barn. Old hay lay strewn over the floor. I can still smell the must and mildew. The glass had been knocked out of the old windows. It was January and so bitterly cold. I tried to sit up, you know, to get off of the floor but I couldn't. I was chained to the floor. I looked all around and found Malin next to me unconscious. Her face was all bloody and her nose was off kilter just enough for me to realize it was broken, like someone had stamped on her face. She was chained to the floor too."

His grip on me doesn't lessen as I try to reach out and touch Malin.

My mind is gone.

"There were three guys, later on a fourth guy came to the barn. They hurt her first. I watched them rape her. Their dicks hanging out of their pants. Hard with excitement, the excitement of our agony. She was screaming. The one who punched me in the parking lot, in the car, Johan was his name. He punched her in the stomach then spread her legs and jammed his dick inside her. He took it right out and showed her blood on it. He was laughing to the other guys that she was a virgin, that he fucked the virginity right out of her, he said. Peter jumped on me thinking I was a virgin too. He shoved my legs apart and rammed his penis into me. He ripped me apart. I was screaming and he seemed to just get off on it. He smelled of sweat and dirt. I can still smell it." I gag as the memory of an odor comes back. "And he was angry I wasn't a virgin. I lost that to a boy at summer camp when I was sixteen. I'd only had sex one time before the kidnapping." I shake my head side to side in disbelief.

"Minutes, hours dragged by as they raped us again and again. I could feel the blood on my legs, pooling beneath my bottom. Emil, the third guy, he shoved his penis in Malin's mouth as Johan raped her. They were laughing about it when another guy showed up. They'd called and invited him over. Max was his name, Max was a sadistic motherfucker. He wore these heavy black steel toe boots."

I can feel my t-shirt dampen on my shoulder and I slump backwards slightly, "Emil tried to shove his penis in my mouth and I bit him on the leg. It wasn't a very good bite. Just a nip but it was enough to really piss off Max. He had them pull my legs hard so I was stretched out, my hands chained above my head and he kicked me in the face." I gently take Will's hand. He releases the vice grip but keeps his other arm around me. I touch his fingers along my jaw near my left ear, "Feel that, right there?" He nods feeling the hardened tissue that lies under my skin so I say, "That's where my jaw dislocated. It hung open for days.

"Max beat me, kicked me," I drag his hand along the left side of my chest. "He broke three of my ribs with his boots." I stare into the past. "Malin tried to stop them. Chained up and she was still a fighter. She was screaming and kicking."

Tears are pouring from my eyes but I keep going, finding strength for my voice, in my words, "He found a broom and broke the handle over his knee. The other guys held her down and he beat her with it.

133

I could hear her bones cracking, breaking as he beat her with the handle. She rolled onto her side one time, trying to get away and he hit her with it really hard in the back. I heard her spine break." Demons, they were demons. They've haunted my mind for years. I let them have control far too long and swallow down my need to vomit at the fear of a memory.

"Max drew back when he broke her spine. He ordered the others out of the barn and left. I think he hoped we would die during the remainder of the cold night. I couldn't reach Malin, my hands," I shake my head, scattering the thoughts. "I tried to touch her with my legs. I managed after a few tries to get closer. She said she couldn't feel my touch. I couldn't talk to her. The pain in my jaw was devastating, and it just hung...wrong.

"When the daylight arrived so did the four men. They were back to see if we died. We disappointed them. They spent the day raping us, beating us then left us again that night. I prayed I would die. I'd never been in so much pain. I was bleeding. I was losing my mind. I wanted death, I begged for it. I begged that every beat of my heart would be the last. Malin was so quiet, I thought she had died a few times during the night but occasionally she would moan. I felt helpless, discarded.

"The next day came and I had managed to sit up. I was pulling on my chains. Picking at the bindings with my bloody fingers. I couldn't get them loose, not

Katherine McLellan

even a little so that I might have been able to wiggle out of them. They wouldn't budge. The men came back and found me. One of them grabbed my leg and pulled me hard, forcing me down again. Max started kicking me," I take Will hand again and move it lower to my hip. "He snapped my pelvis with a kick. I was screaming and cursing but the words wouldn't form because of my jaw. When Max broke my hip the other guy, Emil, pulled at the same time. I pull Will's arms closer, "He yanked my leg right out of the joint."

I feel Willem's tears against my back but I can't stop, not yet when I'm so close to excising the demons from my mind. "Malin started screaming again at them. Johan beat her then Peter raped. It was the last time. She died right then and I couldn't fight for her. She fought to save me but I couldn't do anything to help her. Something in her ruptured, she bled to death on the floor of that barn."

I take a gulp of air and continue, "When they realized what they'd done all four of them turned to me. I was still alive, I was a witness. Max raped me with the broom handle but I really think he was just trying to kill me with it. Peter went for psychological damage and kept telling me that they would find me, that they would track me down and hurt me again. He said I would never be alone. They would always be with me. He was right. They've been with me every day since. Emil must have gotten fed up because he and Johan left. I never saw them again.

"I must have blacked out for a little while because I don't remember Peter and Max leaving. When I woke I tried to get to Malin, where they left her but I couldn't move that far. I couldn't feel parts of my body. My mind was the only thing going. I could hear them all, every one of them burrowing into my brain like cockroaches. I could feel their ghosts touching me, breaking me, leeching onto me. Malin's voice joined them, screaming at them, at me, telling me it was my entire fault."

"Enough," Willem warns. His voice is strong but hoarse and he twists me around. I'm sitting face to face with him; he shifts my legs to lay over his. He wipes his face, getting rid of his tears. If only it was that easy for me. He pulls me into an embrace but I feel numb, empty. I cannot even lift my arms.

I recognize that I cannot stop yet; he needs the whole truth, not just the worst parts of it. I lean back from him and keep going, "I remember the shining beams of light when the police entered the barn. It was like a sliver of hope, light in the dark. They came right to us and checked us. One officer removed his glove and felt my neck. He didn't think I was alive. I must have been too cold, or just, too close to death to distinguish. They were ashamed of the mess we had been left in. The officer laid his jacket over me, I remember the coroner telling him off for compromising the evidence. I was evidence. My body must have spasm right about then. The coroner knelt over me and put a light to my eyes. When they dilated he started screaming for the paramedics. I was life-flighted to Stockholm."

He nods but he doesn't have any words to comfort me. "When I woke they were bringing me into the emergency room. The doctors and nurses, everyone was rushing around. They strapped my wrists to the metal bars of the bed. I'm sure they had a good reason but it's not like I was moving or getting up to leave. I'd spent days bound to the floor and they...restrained me to a bed."

"Assholes," Will mumbles. He gets up from the floor, bends down and picks me up. My legs won't hold any weight so he lifts me like Rhett Butler and carries me back into the bedroom. He sets me on the bed and moves my iPad from where I had left it. He settles me into the bed and embraces me. Together, we lie there.

My sad hazel eyes looking into his sad smoky-blue ones.

I thought he would have left, or at least kicked me out since it is his house. I don't know how he can want me now. My body and mind are broken in so many different pieces and they have been left shattered for years like an undiscovered ancient vase. Unfixable, that's what I am.

"My parents didn't come back for me," I say softly. "I had no visitors except for the police who guarded my door. I was in the hospital for two week. I had four surgeries, an initial one to stop the bleeding that the men and the broom handle had caused. One to fix my jaw. My ribs were left to heal themselves over time. Two other surgeries to repair the damage the men did to my lower half. My pelvis and leg were fixed. Another doctor tried repair the damage to my girlie parts. He tied things that were torn back together. He tried to make me whole but the damage was done." I take Will's hand in mine and place it under my pajama shorts and make him feel the last scar, the one that's in my bikini area. "The doctor said that I could never have children. He said that my uterus could not sustain life." For a long time Will's hand lays over my belly.

Finally I break the silence and say, "They took everything from me: my youth, my sanity, my future."

Chapter 11

I release his hand but it stays where I have placed it. "I would never take your future from you Willem."

"You are my future." It's a profound statement and one I never thought I'd hear but deep down, I know he's wrong.

For a long time we're silent. My past has slammed into our futures in a relentless and unforgiving way. I feel better though. Better than I have felt in over a decade.

"At the hospital," I continue, "the policeman who couldn't find my pulse came to see me. His name is Officer Albinsson. I ended up calling him LT. He told me that they had tried to reach my parents. They had tried to reach my brothers. All of them without success. He said that they had arrested three of the men but that Max was still a fugitive. The men plead guilty to their crimes. I didn't need to give a statement; there was so much physical evidence and then their confessions. LT said I didn't need to speak of it, of the horrors that happened to us in that barn. When I was released from the hospital he drove me to the apartment and told me that I should watch myself, be extra cautious because of Max. The police couldn't provide me with protection after I left the hospital."

"Where were your parents?" he asks.

"Cape Town, but it doesn't matter," I can see the confusion on his handsome face even in the darkness, "I couldn't sleep once I got back to the apartment. I felt like someone was standing behind me, breathing on me. I could feel the men touching me when I was completely alone. I was afraid to be by myself. I would hide in a closet or behind the furniture and nap, five or ten minutes at a time. Every few days Officer Albinsson would come see me, after work before he'd go home to his family. He checked under the beds, the locks on the windows for me and then I'd sleep while he watched TV or just hung out." Willem caresses my face with his fingertips and I lean into him, "It was two weeks before I saw Mrs. Persson." I swear I hear him curse under his breath and I lean away.

"She knocked on my apartment door. It took a few minutes to get to the door since I was still on crutches from my hip surgery. When I opened the door I started to go to her but she was...like ice. She wasn't smiling or happy to see me. All of the love she had ever felt for me was gone. The woman who was so much like a mother to me didn't want me either, like my family.

"We shared the worst kind of loss. I just wanted to be in her arms, to tell her how sorry I was, and am," I choke back the emotions. "She held out her hand and stopped me. She didn't want to touch me. She told me that the thought of touching me was like acid in her mouth."

She said, "You are no child of mine. I've had to bury my child. You did this to her, if it wasn't for you Malin would be alive."

"The voices whispered to me right then, telling me that she was right. They've been with me since. I rocked back on my crutches, stunned by her cruelty but she kept going." I'm weeping again in Will's arms but for a different kind of loss, "She told me to leave, that I was an American, not Swedish, there was no place for me in Stockholm. She wanted me gone and then she turned and walked back into her apartment."

I wipe the tears off with the back of my hand. "I had already been accepted to Cornell. I had enough credits to graduate school even though I'd missed a lot of time. They graduated me earlier, due to the...circumstances."

I feel a little braver so I continue, "She asked me to leave. She told me she didn't want me around. I told Officer Albinsson what I was going to do and he agreed. He thought I would be safer in America since the police were having a hard time finding Max. Three weeks later when I was off of my crutches, I packed a bag and left. I locked up the apartment and have never been back. I'll never go back."

"Why do you say it doesn't matter that your parents were in South Africa? Where were your brothers?"

"Chuck was in jail in Mississippi, it was for a DUI." I'm thinking out loud, "No, that time it was for hitting his ex-wife. My other brother, Trevor, he was on a business trip overseas so he didn't even get the message that the police were looking for him." Willem looks as if he's going to say something and I hold up my hand stopping him, "I didn't speak to them as I grew up. It doesn't matter that they weren't there for me. I don't speak with them now but my parents were different. They should have come but they didn't. I knew exactly where I ranked with them when I left Stockholm. I never spoke with them again. I disconnected my emotions from them. Any feelings I had for them, for my family, I turned off. My father did call once but I refused to speak with him. I had been on my own really, since I was nine. I accepted that years ago.

"My mother died a few years later, when I was in college. My father shortly after. I was notified of their deaths by their attorney. He told me that a trust had been set up for me. My parents knew their mistakes. They knew the incident, the attack, had broken me, mentally. All of my expenses, my college were paid out of the trust. They left me the apartment in Stockholm, and the apartment expenses are paid out of the trust, you know the cleaning, the insurance, and stuff like that. Same for the apartment in New York. Chuck and Trevor got money from their estate. When I turn thirty, whatever's left in the trust will be cashed out and the proceeds sent to me along with the deeds to the properties. I guess they thought I would feel better, mentally, when I turn thirty."

"You still own the apartment in Stockholm?" I nod and he asks, "Why don't you sell it? If you're not going back, why not?"

"I'm not allowed to, my birthday's in November so it's technically owned by the trust, for now, for another year." Since I just sharing everything I say, "You should know, my parents left me a lot of money."

"I don't want to know," he says adamantly.

"I've spent only a little of the money I've made from my books. Mostly on fancy shoes and clothes," I smile weakly.

He places his hand loosely over my mouth, "Stop, I don't need to know about your money." He replaces his hand with a kiss. "All of those bad things. No one should have to go through that," he says sadly, "please tell me something good. What's your happiest memory from childhood? Tell me something good happened to you."

I think for a moment and am relieved to finally smile, "When I was fifteen Malin's family took me to a wedding, out in the country. A cousin of hers was getting married. The celebration lasted three days at an old estate. It was beautiful there, a big old stone house, looking out onto the archipelago. In the morning when the fog would roll into the estate it was so quiet and peaceful. I loved that. I rode a horse for the first time, played on the small beach, in the woods around the estate. I think it was the first time I acted my age. I was so happy there, surrounded by my surrogate family, feeling loved and welcomed."

"That sounds good, sounds like they took good care of you."

"Tell me your happiest memory."

He chuckles quietly, "Oh...that involves my dad and two ducks. I'll tell you later. Please rest Lauren."

I scoot closer and tuck myself into his arms, and lay my head on his chest. The rhythmic movement of his chest and his breathing cocoon me and sleep comes within minutes.

My hand reaches out and finds only emptiness. I wake slightly and hear his quiet voice somewhere else in the house. He's speaking Swedish. That can only mean that he's on the phone with someone far away. I leave the warmth of the bed and walk to the bedroom door. I hate to eavesdrop but that's what sneaky people do.

He's talking and I'm listening, "Hey man, how are you? And Tippy?" Silence, "Good. I'm sure she's busy. Yeah, I know I don't call enough. I can use some advice. I don't know what to do." A half-hearted laugh, "Advice from my younger brother, yeah."

I really wish he'd put it on speaker phone then I could find out which brother he's talking to and what the guy's saying.

"I've started dating someone. She's great, she's smart and beautiful and funny. I think I'm in love with her," my heart soars, "but she's messed up." Aw, the ugly truth. My heart sinks like a fucking stone thrown into a raging river. He agrees with me about my mental status.

Another half-hearted laugh, "Yeah, aren't we all? She was a victim of a violent crime," I've had enough and walk out to him. He doesn't need to talk about that with anyone. I told him all those things in confidence. It's not up to him to tell anyone about what happened to me. I cross my arms over my chest and scowl at him. "And, apparently she doesn't like to be called a victim," he says when he sees how pissed I am. I step closer and motion for the phone, "She wants to talk with you," he hands it over.

"Your brother's an asshole," I say in English glaring at Willem and hand it back before I stomp into the bedroom and slam the door closed because I am that immature and petty.

Several minutes tick by before he comes back to bed. He's gone just long enough for me to get really pissed and then for all the energy to be sapped from me. Disappointingly, I'm not angry anymore as he snuggles up, wrapping his arms around me pulling my back to his chest. He kisses my ear, knowing full well that I'm awake and waiting. I should lay into him, rip him a new one for talking about me. Instead, I'm quiet and he kisses my hair as I say, "I assume that brother was not the architect."

He chuckles, "No, I don't need advice about building you a house." He rolls me over to look at him, "You're not going to like this but when I need help I ask my family. When it comes to you I don't want to do something wrong or say something that will hurt you more than you've already been."

"What did your brother say?"

"He likes people who say what they think, so he likes you already."

I smile in the dark, in his arms.

"Even if you had never been attacked, you'd be fucked up."

"Is that your brother's professional opinion?"

"No, that's my opinion." He looks me in the eyes, "You have a shitty family, Lauren. No one should leave a nine year old girl to grow up alone."

"I did fine on my own," I say defensively.

He gives me a 'don't be stupid look' that instantly softens, "For the most part, yes, you did but you shouldn't have had to. You were a child. You needed your parents like all little kids do. You needed to have your mom tuck you in at night and for your dad to lock the door and keep you safe. You managed it but it should never have been your responsibility." He takes a breath, "There, that's what I have to say about your family. My brother said to tell you how I feel. That's a good place to start."

Chapter 12

"Morning, beautiful," Willem says with a kiss.

I stretch and argue that the new day has not yet started. I open my eyes and find him sitting on the edge of the bed with my iPad in his hands. Talk about snooping. I'm the only one of us allowed to do that. I belly crawl over to his side of the bed and lay there glowering at him for the massive intrusion into my privacy. Oooh, maybe he's a corporate spy getting his hooks into my new book. I blink my eyes awake, doubting very much that Willem is anything except what he claims to be, a good guy with a fucked up lover.

"If you need the password for my bank account, its 3...7...," he leans to me and presses a deep kiss parting my lips so I can't talk. I roll onto my back and smile at him. "Whatcha doing?" I ask, sounding very much like a teenager.

"I needed to see what you're schedule's like for today."

I take the iPad from his hands and push it onto his nightstand. He doesn't need to know what the calendar shows. I am the master of my own domain, "I'm all yours, baby."

A grin spreads across his face, "Good, get up, get dressed. Casual clothes. I have somewhere to go and I want you to go with me."

I end up wearing my favorite jeans and a loose necked beige sweater. It keeps sliding off my shoulders, showing off the camo-colored camisole I'm wearing underneath as I roll down the window of the old truck, laughing at him. Sure his other car is a Maserati but...it's like a bad bumper sticker saying. The truck is so old I don't think it can keep up with the other vehicles on the freeway. The mechanism for rolling the windows down is almost as old as I am.

The wind is blowing through the cab of the truck as we drive along the highway, heading into the city center. My hair is back in a braid which won't last long with the breeze. Will has his aviator sunglasses on and he looks HOT with the wind mussing his golden-brown hair. He's wearing another V-neck t-shirt, navy blue this time and soft, worn jeans. Other cars are zipping past us proving my old truck theory.

The morning sun is shining bright, warming us. It's going to be a good day. It just has that feel. He stretches his hand to mine and holds it as he drives. He knows exactly where he's going and exits off the freeway along a road that directs us towards downtown. At red lights he leans to me and kisses my lips. He reminds me at every opportunity that I'm the most beautiful woman he's ever met. I blush under the weight of compliments.

I'm hoping for more red lights but eventually he signals and turns left when traffic clears. The buildings in this part of town are old, rundown and spray painted. I wouldn't venture here after dark with a new can of pepper spray and a guard dog. There's a large metal fence around the property but the gate is open that secures the parking lot, which is where he parks.

"Take your purse," he says to me rolling up his window. I mimic his movement and in a solid minute of exertion I have the passenger side window up. "I'll call about the car window today. Maybe I can get someone out to the house later to replace it." I scoot out of the truck and shut the door with a loud slam. I swing my purse over my shoulder and take his hand when he comes round the end of the truck. He's smiling as he leads me across the parking lot. "If you get hungry, there's a donut shop down the street." He points back to the right, "Over there. You ready to get your animal instinct on?" He's laughing and walking towards the one entrance, it's got to be the back door to the building or it's the ugliest front door I've ever seen. Plain, steel gray with colorful spray paint all over it. It's hanging slightly open as Will pulls the handle and allows me to step in first.

I am immediately swallowed into darkness as he steps in beside me and closes the door. He takes my hand and leads me down the hallway following the tunneled light. The hall opens into a big, florescent-lit sitting area with an overstuffed brown couch and a few hard plastic chairs. A group of three guys are sitting around talking. They look up at Willem and their conversation quiets. "Mister *Rysberg*," one says embellishing Will's last name. He rises from the couch to shake hands. Like the building, he's a little rough looking with a long gray beard and a beer belly under his straining gray t-shirt.

Will releases mine just long enough to shake hands and introduces me, "Hi Jason, this is my girlfriend Lauren. Lauren, this is Jason Gagnon, master sound producer."

I offer my hand and he accepts with a light squeeze. "I won't take too much of his time young lady. We just need him to redo a few lines for the movie track."

"Okay," I say with no idea of what he's talking about. The other men get up and follow the three of us down the hall to a different set of rooms. I lean to Willem and ask, "What movie?"

He smiles and I'm all gooey again, "I'm in an animated movie. The studio's trying to get it out for Christmas. I'm the voice of the moose." His smile reaches his eyes and I'm stunned by the view. The florescent lighting has turned his eyes dark blue like sapphires twinkling for me.

I don't understand what he sees in me. My freckled short self compared to his Adonis. How I could have gotten so lucky to even spend time with him?

He's really happy about this movie and I'm really happy for him. "It's a great kids movie about a little bear that gets lost in the woods. I can't wait for it to be released. Lucas and Elias have already said they'll take the kids to see it."

He leaves me with the crew of men and follows Jason into the recording studio. One wall is completely glass allowing us to see in, and the actors or whomever is recording to see out. Flat screens are hanging on two of the walls and Will is standing in the middle of the soundproof room. There's a microphone on a tall stand behind a modified laptop in front of him.

The men settle themselves in front of intricate equipment. I have no idea how it works or how to run it. I doubt I could even find the on button. One of the men flips a switch and I can hear Jason and Willem in the other room. Another switch and the animated movie begins to play on the flat screens.

The man running the movie snippets leans forward and presses a button, "Hey Will, we'll get started in a minute. The lines will come up on your laptop. The movie's going to run as well. It'll coordinate with the lines we need redone."

"Sure, sounds good," Will says from within the other room while Jason closes the door behind him and sits down at the machinery.

I take a seat at the far wall, watching them work. I count out the men who are working on a Friday morning. Working with my boyfriend, I almost giggle at the idea. There are the three men plus Will and me. I look around, there's no coffee, no food. I stand up and announce, "I'll go get some coffee for everyone." Jason looks over his shoulder and thanks me. I do charades with Will, rubbing my belly (the universal sign for hunger) and pointing out of the room. He smiles and nods. Tossing my purse over my shoulder I head back the way we came in. Even without a roadmap or GPS I manage to find my way out into the parking lot and out the gate.

It's a quick walk to the donut shop, literally called The Donut Shop. If there was a Shangri La of donuts, it would be this place. My eyes almost close in pleasure as I take in the heavenly scent. Tidy and clean, it's a small shop with only enough space to fit the four tables that are near the front by the large windows.

I groan as I see who's occupying one of the tables. Internally I start looking for my brave face. I courageously walk up to Ethan's table. He innocently looks at me with powdered lips. I step to closer and put my hands on my hips, giving him my bitch face, "If you're stalking me, I'm going to have my boyfriend kick your ass." Best use of boyfriend threat EVER.

He puts his hand to his heart as if I've wounded him. He licks the powder from his lips and says, "Not stalking you. I'm eating a donut. This is the best place for donuts in LA. Is Willem your boyfriend now? That was quick."

"You broke the car window. You're an ass."

I turn my back on him and get back in line as he calls out, "Great ass."

I glance over my shoulder and give him my best I Hate You look. He wipes his mouth with a paper napkin and stands. He's grinning at my anger as he leaves.

I stand in line as people come and go, waiting until the lady behind the counter asks me what I'll have. "I want three dozen donuts," I say, "a variety is fine. I'm going to need five coffees to go. Oh, and a bottle of water." Just in case Will doesn't want anything hot to drink while he's working. She passes over the bottle of water and I shove it in my purse. I pay with my card and put it back quickly. I don't want to hold up the line. She puts four of the coffees in a cardboard tray and stacks the three boxes in a plastic bag. I hang the bag over my good arm. I look at the daunting task of the coffee and grab up the tray in one hand and the other cup in my other hand. It's hot, even with the cardboard sleeve on it. Some guy opens the door for me and I start walking back towards the recording studio.

"Hey pretty lady," he says, "you have your hands full." I turn and look at him. I'm going to say something bitchy to him but he's got a little handheld camera up and running. I can tell by the little red light on it. "Where are you heading?"

Great...first Ethan and now fucking paparazzi. Did he actually recognize me? Or is this just a bored guy's way to eat up time?

"You were on the Late Show the other night, how's the arm?"

Damn, I have been recognized. "It's doing fine." He's walking with me and since it's a free country we can share concrete without it being a crime.

"That's a lot of donuts, are you hungry?"

I really want to screw with him. "Yes, I am very hungry. And thirsty too," motioning to the cups of coffee. "If I start cursing at you, will you have to bleep it all out?" I ask.

"For TV they'll have to but if we put it on the internet and you can curse your head off," he chuckles. He's watching me through the little digital screen. He's not paying any attention to where he's walking, just following me. "Did it hurt when you cut your arm?"

"Well, that's a fucking stupid question," I smile thinking of how much Anne is going to love this impromptu interview. The thought pops into my mind, instead of being bitchy and mean what would the opposite do?

I stop walking and say, "Here hold these for a minute." I pass over the tray of coffee cups and shift the plastic bag. It's hanging awkwardly on my arm, putting ripples in my skin from the weight. I pull out a box and pass it to him as well. We switch, I take back

154

the coffee and say, "That's for you and your friends. Can't have you passing out from hunger if a real celebrity comes by." His head leans slightly to the side, as if I've done something unheard of and alien. His camera hangs low. The little red light has gone off. Mission accomplished.

I set the coffee down first on the little table behind the guys and offer them one of the donut boxes. I start passing out coffee cups, carefully setting it near their equipment. I take the water bottle from my purse and hold up one of the coffees smiling to Willem through the glass window. I'm still laughing at the guy's reaction to the donuts. He points to the water bottle and I ask Jason if I can take it to him. He says it's okay so I let myself into the room and pass it over with a quick kiss.

"Why the big smile?" Will asks quietly.

"I'll tell you later," I'm still grinning as I step out of the room and close the door behind me. I poke around the donuts and take one with colorful sprinkles. I sit to the back of the room and watch as Willem gets animated with his lines. It's so much fun watching the movie on the flat screens when the moose speaks and his voice comes from it. I decide to go see the movie too when it comes out.

It's an hour later when Will is finished. He grabs a box of donuts on the way out and says our goodbyes to the men who have more work to do. Walking into the parking lot we head for the old truck. "So why all the grinning?" he asks as soon as we get into the truck. He picks a donut and shoves half of it into his mouth. I buckle up and tell him of the cameraman and the donuts. He swallows hard and says, "You're telling me you fed the scum of the Earth?"

"I, er, um," I feel suddenly embarrassed, I hadn't thought of him as that.

Willem breaks into a sugary grin, "It's okay, you're a much better person than I am." He backs out of the space then pulls into traffic. I look back to the sidewalk in front of the building and see the paparazzo standing there, watching us leave the recording studio. The young man I'd given the donuts to keeps his camera lowered and walks away. A rush of relief comes over me realizing Willem and I won't be on the internet within the next few minutes.

"I ran into Ethan at the donut shop." I crinkle an eyebrow hesitantly waiting for his response.

"You should have told me that at the studio." He doesn't look happy. "He was an asshole to you and he broke my car. I'll kick his ass the next time I see him." He makes it seem like a promise.

Will pops the last of the donut into his mouth and swallows. He tries to lay his hand on my favorite jeans and I grab it. "Not with all this powder on your fingers." I lean to his hand and suck each finger clean, swirling my tongue around each digit. I lean back and pronounce him, "Yummy."

He whispers, "Wow," and shakes his head to clear the cobwebs. "I was going to take you to the park but I'm thinking we should just go home and spend all day in bed covered in donut powder." I'm staring at him blankly, was that a choice for today?

"I choose donut powder," I declare with utmost certainty.

"Nice try, beautiful. I'm taking you to the park." I stick my bottom lip out and pout. Next red light he leans to me and nibbles on my lip. I'll have to remember to pout more often.

We get back onto the freeway and he drives north for a while. With no red lights our drive is almost tame. His hand squeezes my thigh and I look at him. Mr. Hotty McHotpants with those sexy aviator glasses on wants my attention. He distracts me by shifting slightly and taking his wallet from his back pocket. He hands it to me and says, "Get out twenty five, babe."

He's slowing down the old truck for a toll booth. I'm thinking it's an expensive toll when I realize he's exited the freeway and the toll booth really isn't a toll booth. It's the main gate for an amusement park. I open the soft leather wallet and extract the correct bills. While it's open I poke my finger around considering the contents. Satisfied that there's nothing out of place in his wallet like some young ho's phone number I hand it back to him.

He shakes his head at my obvious snooping and rolls down the window. He tucks the wallet into his back pocket and tells the attendant, "Premier parking." The bills are handed over and a neon green pass is given. He hands it to me as if I'll know what to do with it. I'm holding it as if it contains the Ebola virus, pinched between two fingers and slightly away. He rolls up his window and takes the pass from me since I've made no move to do anything with it.

"No amusement parks in New York?" He hangs the pass from the rearview mirror and continues along the park road towards the parking lot.

"I don't get out much." It would just be too expensive to go to a park and pay for me and the five other people in my head.

He gets a really good parking space but then I remind myself that's what he's paid for. I don't want to take my purse into the park and have to carry it around all day. I start digging through it for my ID and a credit card. He's watching me with a wistful, yet patient smile on his face as I lean forward and shove my purse under the seat. "Don't let me forgot those later," I say to him as I pass them over. He sticks them in his wallet for care and safe keeping.

I dangle the neon pink plastic wristlet and give it a spin. It has the look of a hospital tag but I've never seen them in neon colors. "So, what's this do for us?" I ask. He takes my hand and leads me away from the ticket stand.

"These are line-cutter passes." That sounds very fourth grade. "No matter the size of the line we get to go first on any of the rides." The pink wristlet looks better on his wrist than mine.

"Because you paid for it?"

"Yes," he smiles and gives my hand a squeeze. "Do you like rollercoasters?"

"I don't know. I haven't been on any." He looks at me like I've had an alien baby burst through my chest wall. "You know my family never took me on vacation."

"What about school field trips or college? You had to go to a park during college."

I shake my head, taking in the park. It's much greener than I thought it would be with lots of tall trees. There's a theme of medieval castles and fake facades that mirror the time period. "Field trips were to historical places, do real castles count?" I smile as we continue walking. "College, well, that was full of schoolwork and alcohol." He smiles like he doesn't believe me so I admit, "OK, lots of schoolwork and not much alcohol."

"Come on then, let's break your duck." He tugs my hand leading me away from the main walking path into the first rollercoaster entrance.

There are screams from up high so I lift my head and watch the riders who are suspended in the air, hanging over the edge of the coaster. I count to three and it releases, dropping the people and their screams into hyper-speed then a corkscrew. He tugs on my hand and gets me walking again. I just can't believe we're going to do that in a minute.

With our neon pink passes we indeed cut the line. I'm strapped into the front row, right next to Willem. An attendant comes by and pulls hard on my safety harness. I give it a tug too, just to make sure. I grip the metal handles hard, not really knowing what to expect. The attendants check everyone behind us and I can see when they give a thumbs up signal. The coaster jerks awake and pulls us out of the little stationhouse. It's a slow climb upward and I tilt my head over to Will. He's got on a cheese-eating grin and I'm suddenly worried.

The coaster rolls over the smooth metal track around a little bend, way...up...high then it stops. The front row, meaning me and Willem are hanging over the ground. The track is nowhere to be seen. My heart is racing with panic. I'm dangling. The harness is the only thing keeping me from falling. It's a very long way down to the sudden stop of ground and concrete. Screams start from behind me and my adrenaline spikes. Just when my heart steadies I'm dropped like a fucking stone. I'm screaming and death-gripping the metal handles as I'm flipped into the corkscrew, upside down then around. The wind's rushing through my hair as we flip again and I'm still screaming. A few more loops and turns and I stop screaming and start laughing before we pull into the little station house. I'm wearing the same cheesy grin I'd seen on Willem's face earlier.

I nearly hop out of the seat as soon as the attendant releases me. I'm so wound up. I take Will's hand and lead him from the building. "That was awesome!" I'm grinning and excited, "I want to ride all of the roller coasters!"

"Excellent," he says like Dr. Evil.

The morning and afternoon fade away into the screams and laughter of having fun. We walk the whole park; ride all of the coasters, some three or four times. I look up at him and ask, "Can we do one more thing?" He immediately agrees though I haven't even told him what I want. "I don't know how far away it is, but can we go watch the sunset at the beach? I've never seen the sun set over the ocean before." He presses a kiss to my hand and we walk back to the truck.

In the cab of the truck, I nibble on my bottom lip, hesitant and undecided about something.

"What's up, beautiful?" he asks sensing my mood shift.

I look over at him and slide closer along the bench seat. My arm hooks around his neck bringing him to eye level. I'm very serious as I say, "Thank you for today. I've had so much fun with you." I press a passionate kiss to his lips. I shift and sit up on my knees, wrapping my other arm around his neck. He returns my passion with just enough tongue in his kiss to heat up my insides.

"Lauren," he says through the kisses, "we can't here. We're in a parking lot." His hands hold my hips firmly, pushing me slightly back. I'm clinging to him like he's a life preserver. I'm sure my kisses can keep him close. He lays me back along the seat and hovers over me. One of my legs wiggles its way past the steering wheel and I pull him to me with my foot. I can feel his erection through our jeans. It gives me a joyous feeling to know the affect I have on him.

He smiles, his hand running along my leg. "If only you hadn't worn jeans," he says with a devious smile. "I'd take you here and now, no matter whose camera is recording." He sits up, leaving me hot and bothered on the bench seat. He pats my leg and starts the truck.

Willem drives to the beach, but not anywhere near the pier where we had gone that first night. Our first night, it feels so long ago. I don't understand how in just a few days I've fallen in love with this beautiful man, who wants me, no matter what demons lay inside. Instead of the raucous pier, he takes me somewhere quiet, out of the way.

The roadside parking lot is empty except for his truck. We walk a little distance to find the sandy path to the coast. As soon as we reach sand I stop and remove my shoes. Willem takes a knee and rolls my jean legs up to avoid sand. My hand falls to his muscular shoulder and again I'm in awe of this man. He's always thinking about things I might need. *Has anyone ever done that?* I wonder to myself. Standing from my jeans he takes my hand again and leads me along the path.

Our forgotten piece of the world is unobtrusive and bathed in oranges and yellows as Willem sits behind me, holding me close; his long legs go well past mine as I dig my toes into the warm, sun soaked sand. His arms drape over mine and I lean my head against his bicep. He presses a soft kiss to my neck and says quietly, "I want to give you the world, Lauren."

"You have," I answer softly. "This beach is the most peaceful thing anyone's ever given me. And the rollercoasters were the most fun!"

"The most fun?" he asks nibbling on my neck.

I break into a grin, "Well, maybe not the most fun," I silence a giggle.

He's given me so much more than just the secluded beach and rollercoasters over our days together. To have received a lifetime of love in days,

163

how many people can make that claim? I am so lucky to have met him. Feelings and desires that I never knew existed; he's brought those out in me, all for better. These are gifts he's given me, precious memories, feelings that will linger all my life.

He leans his chin on my shoulder and I press my hand against his face. Is this how lovers act? Aren't we supposed to take care of one another? Save the best of one's life and then give it to another? What if I don't have anything good to give him?

His arm shifts to my waist and he holds me close. Leaning back I press into him. Watching the sun sink over the Pacific I wonder if it's selfish for me to want him, to need the world he wants to give me. I should let him find someone else to love, someone who's healthy and whole. He needs someone who doesn't look at a sunset and see an end, rather than the possibilities of what a new beginning could bring.

I turn in his arms and inhale with adoration at his beauty in the sunset. His blonde hair is nearly golden, his eyes more gray than blue. His fingers touch my face and I lean into his palm. "Is this how love feels?" I ask in a soft voice.

He leans forward and presses a cherished kiss to my lips then says, "Yes, it is."

"You love me?"

"I do, more than you know," he confirms. His fingers push away the loose hair from my face. "I feel like I started to breathe for the first time in my life the day we met." His eyes fall shyly to the sand then return to mine as he declares, "I can be strong for you, I can be the man you need me to be, Lauren."

"You already are." I lean to him and press a kiss to his sundrenched lips. Love? Real love? How could I get so lucky?

Leaning back I hike my sweater off and over my head. I stand and unbutton my jeans as he watches. Just me in my little hunter-green panties and camo shirt. He's smiling again but glancing around our secluded beach nervously. I kick off my jeans and step back from him finding the warm water lapping at my ankles. I reach out a hand for him and motion for him to join me.

By the time I sink into the water he's dropped his shirt and jeans onto the beach and he's with me, left only in his black boxer briefs. "This is not a good idea," he says as his arms wrap around me, holding me up in the water. He nuzzles my neck sending my hoochie into overdrive.

"You have a fear of public sex?" I ask, suddenly aware that he might actually have fears he's never told me of. I may not be the only one afraid of things.

He twists us in the water, moving us further away from shore. "I have a fear of recording devices and the internet." He dunks us under and pops right up. My camo shirt is soaking through revealing my raised, firm nipples. He looks down and smiles. I think he's done that on purpose.

He moves us through the water to a small inlet further along the shore. It's overgrown with trees and beach grass creating a natural tunnel over the warm water. It's sheltered and out of the way, perfect for obscuring the view of lovers and their needs. He presses me back against the warm rocky ledge.

"Can you feel the bottom with your feet?" I ask. He's nestling kisses on my neck causing my heart to race and murmurs, "Mmm," which I take to mean yes to my question. "Do you want to have sex here?" I ask him as his lips move along my chest. He pulls at the neck of my wet shirt and pushes my breasts up revealing the rosy peaks.

His lips and tongue find the firm crests and I melt in his arms. "I don't want to have sex with you, Lauren." I am completely disappointed, crushed against the jagged rocks. "I want to make love to you." My heart skips a beat. He quiets his kisses and says like he's revealing a secret, "I want to make love to you every day of our lives."

His eyes search mine for acceptance and permission, and I give it.

The world just hours before which was immersed in gold and orange is now dark and eerily quiet as I step into the kitchen and find a pen in my purse. I find a piece of scrap paper and write Willem a

166

note, rather than wake him up. I think for a moment then write, 'I'm leaving for New York but my love remains with you.' I sign it Lauren and tuck it under his keys so he'll find it in the morning.

I wheel my black bag to the front door and my heart is breaking. I leave it at the door and tiptoe back to the bedroom. I need to have a last kiss before I never see him again. I told him I would not take his future from him and I meant it but I feel sick, ever doubting myself. I know he needs to find real love, to have children and a future. He won't find that in me.

Quietly I sneak back into the bedroom and lean over him, careful not to fall into him or wake him in some other way with my clumsiness. I press a soft kiss to his lips, "I love you, I always will." I whisper then retreat.

I walk my suitcase and purse down the concrete path from the house and take a seat on the steps to the sidewalk. I'd called a cab hours ago and gave them a designated time to meet. It should be here soon. I'd already delayed my return once.

I'm overwhelmed by my emotions for Willem. I have to go back to New York. I need to leave before I make mistakes that will devastate us both.

There's some movement behind me and my heart lurches. Willem sits down beside me and asks, "What are you doing, Lauren? You're leaving?"

So much for a sneaky escape, "I have a flight to catch. I didn't want the taxi to wake you."

"That's bullshit."

We're quiet for a long time.

"Yeah, I know. It is," I say giving in that I am the weak one and he's strong one of our fucked up relationship.

Willem leans close and takes my hand, "Stay with me." He's almost begging as the taxi arrives, "Give me two more days." He's bargaining, "Come on, Lauren. Give me another day." His voice turns stern, "We need to talk," and then lenient and compassionate, "I love you. I don't want you to go, not like this."

I stand and push my bag towards the taxi. I turn back for him, "I did give you a day and today, ah, yesterday was the best day I've had, maybe ever." The driver gets out and puts my bag in the trunk and then gets back in the car.

I hitch my purse over my shoulder, "I love you, Willem but you deserve," I shrug, "much more than me. I have nothing to offer but my demons." With a heavy heart I turn from him and get into the taxi. I look to him but I don't even have the strength to lift my hand as the taxi leaves. I cannot take my eyes off of him. The image of Willem standing there in the darkened empty world haunts me, crushing my soul, extinguishing any hope that might have remained.

Chapter 13

I've had a bitch of a bad week. The demons I had talked of that last night with Willem have come to settle again. Five voices plus my own, all roosting around in my mind, picking apart each and every decision, action, touch that happened in California are now forcing me to drink and make bad choices in general. It's not enough to have a broken heart; to have five other voices constantly telling me what I did wrong is driving me crazy. Literally.

I have been supporting my broken, lovesick heart with wine and Ho-Hos. I'm sure I've gained weight but since I've made the decision to be a lonely old woman I'm sure no one will notice or care. My next step is to adopt cats.

I must lay with my demons, accept my choice. There won't be any moving on, that would be too hopeful and I don't have any hope left. Not after watching me break Willem's heart as the taxi drove away.

My cell phone rings again and I listen to Anne leave another pissed off message, "Lauren if you don't pick up the phone I'm coming over to your apartment. NOW!" I lean against the kitchen counter and see that she's left many messages today. I did listen to them, I just didn't have the heart to return any of her calls. She keeps telling me it's important, it's urgent, she needs me to call her back right away but I have more wine to drink, more Ho-Hos to eat. I've stopped using a glass, instead chugging from the bottle. I'm a miserable slob, an unhealthy one at that with the amount of chocolate I've eaten over the last nine days.

It's about one in the afternoon when the sound of a knock echoes through my quiet apartment. I'm sitting in my work area in the corner of the apartment, staring out the window at the busy little people moving about below. They look like ants, busy little ants, little ants with hope and contentment of their busy little lives. I hate them.

The knock is demanding so I leave my wine and chocolates on the desk and walk across the living room. I tread along the carpeted hall, slightly buzzed from my alcoholic soaking but find my bare feet are moving one in front of another. I think this is positive, the ability to walk. Another knock so I shout, "Anne keep your pants on." I instantly regret the loud sound and press my hand to my temple.

I pull open the door and Anne is not standing there. My mouth drops open as Willem stands in my doorway. My heart runs back to the living room, throws open one of the windows and jumps. She does not survive the four story fall.

I swallow hard, "Hi," I manage. Suddenly, all of the wine doesn't seem like it's been such a good idea. He's so fucking attractive but now I see more. His soul is beautiful and endearing, wrapped in a fantastic package.

I must be brave, I must be strong I tell myself. I definitely don't want to crack under the pressure of my broken heart. One, two, three...I don't even count to ten before I fall into his arms, instantly crying, "I so sorry!" Well, my determination didn't last long. He's holding me in the entryway of my home. I feel a little kiss to my head before he steps into the apartment with me in tow. The door closes and he stands me up a little so that I'm not leaning so heavily on him.

"Are you drunk?" he asks.

"No, I'm enamored."

"Inebriated?"

"Both?" I question.

He takes my hand and walks me into the living room. I nearly fall into the couch before he stops and looks me over. I'm a hot mess. He looks away from me, taking in my apartment. From the living room he can see my Ho-Ho trash strewn from the work area on one side across the living room to the granite kitchen island where more than a few empty wine bottles stand. There's a smaller bedroom just past the kitchen, but only the doorway is visible.

He says, "I would have come sooner but I was pissed," he stops looking around and turns back to me. I get his point. I left badly. "And it took time to arrange things, to clear my schedule for a while." He steps to the fireplace mantel and picks up a little figurine. The little marble elephant rolls in his fingers before he sets it down, "I'm only here because I have a long layover."

"You're going home?"

"Yes," there's silence as he steps back to me, "come on, you need to get cleaned up." He grabs me under my arms and lifts me from the couch and asks were the bathroom is. I nod to the far door in the living room, close to my work area.

"That's my bedroom," I say pointing to the door. He will be the first man to enter. I don't think deliverymen count.

He takes my hand and leads me into my own room. The bedroom furniture is simple dark hardwood; a big bed, a dresser, a nightstand to match the bed and an antique rocking chair I found at a yard sale. That was a bitch dragging it home. There's a flat screen that one of the deliverymen hung on the wall opposite the bed but I don't watch it often. I point again, giving him direction to my bathroom.

"You should know by now," he says flipping on the bathroom light. "I like to take care of people. I'm the oldest of six. I've been taking care of every one of my siblings for years. If you don't want me to take care of you, tell me." He turns and strips off my t-shirt. I'm standing there, naked as can be on my top half. He turns and starts my shower water. "I like taking care of you." My pajama pants come off next. I feel utterly exposed under his glare. I feel ashamed of how I acted, how I left. Even the fact that I've drunk so much over the last week bothers me on some level. What had helped keep me calm, mellow, now only embarrasses me. He feels the shower water and pronounces it good enough.

I step in as he steps out of the bathroom.

From the shower I can hear the clanking of glass and peek my head out. He's got a trash bag and he's not afraid to use it. I see him wandering my room, picking up things, tossing away those things which he considers trash. I shake my head and return to the hot water. I suppose a tidy man is better than a sloppy one. Oh, does that make me the slob?

I turn off the water and squeeze my hair. I wrap a soft blue towel around my body and another for my hair. I grab my comb on the way out and find him sitting on my bed. The cleaning has finished, my place is tidy again, empty of chocolate wrappers and glass wine bottles.

I sit on the bed next to his shoes and offer him my comb. He accepts and I turn my back to him. He gently removes the towel from my hair and begins to squeeze the water from the tangled mess with it.

He separates my hair into sections and begins to work the comb through it as he continues, "I came to give you back your ID and credit card. You left them at my house." Yes, I know I did. I had a shit of a time getting through airport security when I realized I didn't have them on me that morning. "I set those on your dresser." I glance over and see them there. "I also came to make you an offer." He holds a tangle in front of my face to show me his problem.

"Like *The Godfather*, right?" I ask.

"Yeah, one I'm hoping you won't refuse." He finishes that section of my tangled mess and begins to work another. "I have a five hour layover. I bought you a ticket too. I want you to come home with me." My heart races but I don't say anything. "I want to explain something." He stops combing my hair and turns me around. I'm looking into those stunning eyes, nothing has changed for me. I'm still in love with him, I may be forever.

He says, "I want you. I want to be with you. I'm in love with you, Lauren, but I want someone who wants all of me. I am Swedish, it's my home. If you don't want that part of me, then I'm not willing to give the rest."

His hands run along my freckled arms, to my shoulders, my neck holding me gently as he continues, "I'm willing to give you everything. I can live here. I don't have to live in LA. If you want kids, we can use a surrogate or we can adopt but we don't have to have kids for me to be happy. I'll be happy with just you."

A surrogate? I hadn't thought of that. Could I actually have children with him? A flutter of hope ignites in my chest. He's willing to move here, for me? He leans forward and presses a cautious kiss to my lips.

My dizzying mind begins to spin faster. All that wine was not a good idea.

"It's all or nothing, babe." He kisses me again, more sure of himself and my possible answer. "Will you go home with me? Back to Sweden?" His lips caress mine again.

His kisses become more passionate, first to my neck then my lips. My eyes close in pleasure that I was sure I would never know again. My towel falls around my waist as his hands find my delicate skin. I want him, I want all of him and I push myself up into his lap. I want him to make love to me and return his kisses passionately. His erection is hard beneath me as I straddle him. I'm kissing him, my fingers running through his hair as he holds me close, holds me to him hard. I might hurt him I want him so badly.

"I want you," I whisper through a kiss.

"How much, baby?"

I push at his clothes. I need to get them off. I can only think of one thing. I want him, I want him desperately. His jacket is hurriedly tossed to the floor. He pulls his shirt off and our skin touches. It intensifies my desire and I want more. He rolls on top of me, pulling the towel from between us. His pants and boxer briefs come off in a heated rush.

"How much do you want me, Lauren?" he asks urgently.

I need to think but I can't concentrate. How much do I want him? I realize it's not a matter of want, not anymore. I need him, but enough to go back someplace I'm not wanted?

Willem's gazing into my eyes and I realize I am desired, loved. He needs me to go back with him. He'll take care of me; protect me, even in the dark corners of my mind, the places I fear most. He wants me, all of me, even the crazy parts. My legs wrap around his hips, his erection is teasing me, tempting me with a new promise of love.

I nod and accept he's won again, "I need you," I take a haggard breath, "all of you, every part."

He smiles and whispers, "Victory is mine," as his erection enters my wetness and we melt into one. His strong thrusts are rhythmic and my renewed pleasure is intense before he stops suddenly and looks at me. He's got something to say.

His voice is husky with adoration, "I love you, Lauren. I got your luggage out of the closet while you were in the shower."

I lean my head back over the edge of the bed and see it waiting for me. I look back into those beautiful eyes, "You know, you play dirty."

His smile brightens my world as he says, "All's fair in love."

The End of Book 1

Made in the USA
Charleston, SC
14 October 2012